D1527686

L.H. COSWAY

A

Crack

IN

EVERYTHING

"I'm trying to free your mind, Neo. But I can only show you the door. You're the one that has to walk through it."

- Morpheus, *The Matrix*.

-

One
Inner City Dublin, Ireland. 2006.

Waiting for a flower bud to open was one of my favourite things.

It started out like a closed little pistachio. The next day its petals moved. The following day they spread. The day after that they spread a little bit more, and then finally the flower blossomed to its full potential.

I was waiting for the buds on my pink hibiscus to open, but they still had a few days to go. I poured a little water into the pot with a plastic bottle then screwed the cap back on. I was just about to place it on the shelf when someone hammered on my door.

It was a panicked knock, one that demanded attention. In this neighbourhood, it didn't always bode well to open the door to knocking like that. I squinted through the peephole and recognised a boy I went to school with. His name was Dylan O'Dea, or was it O'Toole? Anyway, I was pretty sure he lived one or two floors below me here at St Mary's Villas.

Don't let the 'Villas' part fool you. There was nothing villa-like about this place. St Mary's War Bunker would've been more apt. Everything was grey. The windows gave the barest minimum of light, and every single flat smelled vaguely of mildew no matter how much you cleaned or aired the place.

Dylan looked sweaty and desperate, and there was something about his panicked gaze that had me unlocking my door for him. Before I even had the chance to say a word, he barrelled in and slammed the door shut behind him.

"What the hell!" I exclaimed, at once regretting my decision. I lived with my aunt Yvonne, but she was at work and wouldn't be home for hours.

Dylan stared me dead in the eye, his chest heaving, and raised a finger to his mouth in the universal gesture of 'be quiet.' I didn't make a peep and a second later noise sounded from outside. People banged on doors the same way Dylan had been banging on mine. Our eyes met again, and he must've sensed I was going to say something because he came at me. He backed me up against the wall until his frame surrounded mine and his hand went to my mouth. I instantly struggled, but then he whispered in my ear.

"Please don't make any noise. Some people are after me. I just need to hide here for a few minutes and then I'll leave. I promise."

I glared at him and lifted my foot to stomp on his ankle. He swore under his breath but didn't loosen his hold.

"Fuck you," I mumbled past his fingers. "Get out!" It sounded more like, "Fup Ooo. Et oot."

"Please, Evelyn. I need your help."

My heart hammered. He knew my name. Although it wasn't so strange since most people knew each other's names around here. It just felt odd for him to address me so familiarly, because we'd never spoken.

The sincerity in his dark blue eyes made me pause in my struggle. We stared at each other for another long moment, and goosebumps claimed my skin. His chest was wide and solid, and he smelled like cloves.

"If I lower my hand, do you promise not to scream?" he asked very quietly.

I nodded slowly, and his hand left my mouth. "Who's after you?" I whispered, worried he'd brought trouble to my door.

"A few lads from the McCarthy gang. They've been trying to recruit me. I told Tommy McCarthy to go fuck off and now they want to give me a hiding."

"Shite," I breathed.

The knocking came closer. Whoever it was reached the flat next to mine and banged on the door. I held still, barely breathing. My eyes traced Dylan's face, his stunning eyes, masculine jaw, and gruff expression. He wore grey jeans, black boots, and a navy padded jacket. His sandy hair was somewhere between blond and brown, and it had a slight curl to it. It was clipped short, so the curl didn't have much room to . . . be curly.

He was very attractive, but that didn't take away from the fact that he'd basically broken into my home. When my neighbour came out and started talking to the lads who were looking for Dylan, I whispered, "Why did you come here to hide?"

He made a thoughtful expression, his brow furrowing in a way that made him look like a grumpy bear. "What?"

"You could've gone into any flat, why this one?"

There was a beat of silence, then finally he whispered back, "Because you're the only person on this row who wouldn't feed me to the wolves."

I arched a brow. "You don't know that."

You don't know me.

Before he had a chance to reply, the banging started on my door. My chest seized, clutched by fear, because I knew the type of blokes who were out there.

Poor. Hard. Brutal.

Suddenly, Dylan was on me again, his hand on my mouth, his body holding mine in place. This time I didn't struggle, instead I held still and stayed quiet. A shiver trickled down my spine at his closeness. I wasn't often this close to people I hardly knew.

"Answer the bleedin' door," a male voice shouted, "or I'll knock it the fuck down."

"Maybe I should answer and tell them you're not here," I whispered against his fingers.

He glanced down at me, probably because my lips were on his skin. He tilted his head, like he found it in some way interesting, then said, "No, they'll come in and ransack the place."

I let out an anxious breath. He was right. And I couldn't do that to Yvonne. I couldn't have her come home from her shift at the bar to a wrecked flat.

More banging ensued. I startled when a head appeared at the window, though thankfully Yvonne's net curtains shielded us from view.

"He's not in there," someone said. "He probably ran down to the Willows."

The Willows was a dilapidated block of flats about five minutes away. It was where people went to drink and do drugs. If you were homeless, it was where you went to sleep.

"Come on," the same person said, and the guy peering in the window disappeared. Dylan let go of me, took three strides across the room and looked out through the curtains.

"They're gone," he said and exhaled, his shoulders slumping in relief.

"Yes, now you should go, too," I said, on guard again. I felt on edge having a strange boy in my flat who I'd never spoken to before. Though 'boy' wasn't exactly the right term. Dylan was probably about a year older than me, eighteen maybe, but he was built like a man. Soon his shoulders would get even broader, his features more defined. He'd be a sight to be reckoned with then, I was sure.

He turned back to look at me, one eyebrow arching as he stared me down. He didn't do anything for a long moment and then his attention moved about the living room. His tension faded, and something like fondness, or maybe amusement, took its place.

"Big fan of New York?" he asked wryly, taking in all the posters and memorabilia.

I cleared my throat. "No, my aunt Yvonne is. She saw *When Harry Met Sally* and became obsessed. She's saving up to move there in a couple years."

Dylan's mouth formed an attractive, thoughtful line. "And what about you?"

"What about me?"

"Will you go with her?"

I shrugged. "I don't think so. Probably not. My grandma lives in the retirement home in Broadstone. We're all she has. I couldn't leave her."

Dylan took this in, his dark eyes softening, then stepped to the front door. "Thanks for letting me hide here. I owe you one," he said, ducking his head to make sure the coast was clear.

"Sure," I said, not knowing what else to say.

He looked back at me one last time. "See ya, Evelyn." And then he was gone.

***

"I'm sorry, but I'd sell my own mother for a night with Jared Leto, no question," said Sam as we walked to English on Monday.

"Are we talking *30 Seconds to Mars* Jared Leto or *Jordan Catalano* Jared?" I asked. "Because those are two entirely different kettles of fish."

"*30 Seconds*, of course. You know I can't resist a man in eyeliner," he said then winked. We reached our lockers when a familiar head of sandy brown hair emerged from the crowd.

Dylan.

He must've sensed my attention, because his gaze flashed to mine. I sucked in a harsh breath at the sight of him. He had a purple bruise beneath one eye, and there were various other cuts and grazes all over his face. Jesus.

Sam followed where my eyes went and made a crass comment. "Looks like Dylan O'Dea likes it rough."

So it was O'Dea.

"I think he got that beating on the streets, not in the sheets," I said, chewing worriedly on my lip. Those McCarthy fellas must've caught up to him yesterday.

"Good one." Sam chuckled, but I didn't share his humour.

A pang of concern hit me square in the chest, and I moved toward him automatically, leaving Sam by his locker. Dylan saw me approach and stopped in place, his attention skittering over me. He hitched his bag on his shoulder and let out a gruff breath. "What?" he asked.

"They got you, didn't they?"

He shifted from foot to foot, seeming uncomfortable with my concern. "Nah, walked into a wall."

"Don't be cute."

Another sigh. "Yeah. They got me, blondie. Probably better to get it over with anyway. Now maybe they'll leave me alone."

I nodded slowly, not sure how to react to his endearment. It wasn't very original, but it still made my breastplate tingle. "You think?"

"I hope, but who knows."

"Have any teachers asked about your bruises?"

He gave me an incredulous look. "Where do you think we are? Nobody gives a shit here."

I hated that he was right. The teachers at this school were either too mean or too downtrodden to care about students' home lives. In a way, I didn't blame them. Even the nice teachers eventually got so sick of being bullied and verbally abused that they shut off all their emotions. This wasn't a soft place to grow up, but I liked to think I still had a heart.

I didn't think before I said my next words. "Well, *I* give a shit."

He narrowed his eyes in suspicion. "Why?"

"Because I'm not an unfeeling rock, that's why."

Dylan stared off over my head and shoved his hands in his pockets. "You probably should be," he said then walked by me and disappeared back into the crowd.

Huh.

"Oh *blondie*, get your bum over here," Sam crooned, and I turned back to my friend.

"What?" I asked.

"I didn't know you and Dylan O'Dea were acquainted."

I frowned. "We're not. Not really."

He folded his arms and pursed his lips. "Sure sounded like you are."

"He was being chased by some blokes who wanted to beat him yesterday, and I let him hide in my flat. That's it."

"Oooh, racy. Did he happen to hide in your bedroom by any chance? And did you share a sexy moment once the coast was clear? How did he express his gratitude?"

Trust Sam to turn everything into some sort of risqué soap opera. Although thinking about it, the way Dylan held his hand over my mouth did give me a flutter in my belly.

"He told me he owed me one," I replied with a shrug. Sam's eyes glittered.

"That means he owes you a good rogering."

"Sam!"

"What?"

"Don't be disgusting."

"Nothing disgusting about sex with a fella like that, Ev. Besides, you need to lose that flower of yours before it shrivels up and dies."

I scrunched my face. "Please don't call it a flower. And anyway, I'm not the only one who needs to lose it, so you can quit talking like you know it all."

He gave me a sassy look. "If I were as straight and as pretty as you are, I'd have lost it years ago. It's not exactly easy to find gays in this neck of the woods."

"Not easy to find gays who are out, you mean. Just wait for the next person who throws some homophobic slur at you, and there's a good chance he's in the closet."

"Hmm, I do get a hint of an angry sex vibe from Shane Huntley sometimes. Maybe you're onto something."

Speak of the devil. A few seconds after Sam mentioned him, Shane walked by with his ever-present posse of arseholes, sneer in place. I wondered why the meanest kids always seemed to have the most friends. I didn't have a mean bone in my body and the only real friend I had was Sam. Shane walked on, not acknowledging us aside from his sneering expression, and I turned to neaten up my locker.

"I found a book on Freud in Yvonne's collection. He had this theory that when we see the things we dislike in ourselves in others, we hate on it."

"Hmm," said Sam. "Could be some truth to it. But anyway, back to the luscious Mr O'Dea, when are you going to cash in on that debt?"

I chuckled. "Not sure. Maybe the next time I need help moving furniture. The boy's got some serious shoulders on him."

"All the better for throwing you around the bedroom with."

I shot him an irritable glance. "You're not going to quit with this, are you?"

His answering wink was pure devilment. "Not in this lifetime, blondie."

Two

"It's a Friday night and yet again, we have nothing to do," Sam declared with a bored sigh as he flopped onto the couch.

"Aren't there any teen discos you two can go to?" Yvonne asked, pulling her hair into a ponytail as she got ready for her shift at the bar.

"There are plenty," Sam replied. "But your niece thinks she's too cool for that sort of malarkey."

"I don't think I'm too cool, I just don't enjoy them. All we do is sit in a corner, waiting for boys to notice us. We don't even dance. What's the point?"

"I promise I'll dance tonight if you come with me," Sam begged as he got off the couch and dropped to his knees.

I lifted a brow. "You're lying. Once we get there, it'll be all 'oh, why don't we just sit for a while' and then before we know it, the thing will be over and no dancing will be had."

Yvonne shot Sam a curious frown. "But you love to dance."

"I love dancing in the privacy of my own home," he pointed out. "I *don't* love dancing in public places, where the cockroaches like to snicker and make fun of me."

Yvonne exhaled a sad breath. "Sometimes I forget how horrible teenagers are. Present company excluded."

"You're only twenty-seven. It's not too long since you were one of them," I reminded her.

Yvonne chuckled. "Thanks for the compliment, but sometimes it feels like I was always this age."

She wasn't lying. Yvonne had taken on adult roles a lot earlier than most, caring for my Gran when she developed MS, and then for me when my mam did a bunk. I brought my attention back to Sam. "Seriously though, you shouldn't let them bully you out of doing something you love. If anyone even so much as looks at you funny, I'll see to them."

Sam made a show of swooning. "My hero. Tell me again why you couldn't have been born with a penis? We'd have made the perfect couple."

"It's God's sick joke, making us soulmates but with the wrong equipment," I said playfully.

"You two are too much." Yvonne shook her head. "Whatever you end up doing tonight, be safe, okay? I'll be home later."

"We will. See you in the morning."

"See you, love," she said and came to give me a kiss on the temple then gave Sam one, as well. I swear, she was more of a mother to us than any of our biological parents. In my case, that was very much true. I'd lived with Yvonne since I was thirteen and my mam decided she was wasting her life taking care of a kid. She left me with her much nicer, much more responsible younger sister and moved to London to live her dream.

Apparently, living her dream involved working in a clothing boutique, wasting all her money on alcohol

20

and her heart on careless men. Every time she called she seemed to have a new boyfriend on the go, but there was no talking to her. In truth, I preferred it this way. My life was so much more stable living with Yvonne than it had ever been with Mam.

I looked to Sam. "I guess if we're really doing this I should get changed."

"Oh no, pyjama pants and stained T-shirts are the go-to outfit for discos these days," he said sarcastically.

I threw a pillow at him and got up to shuffle into my room. In the end, I went with a tight black mini dress, lace-patterned tights, ankle boots, and a denim jacket. Sam was already wearing jeans and a shirt, so he didn't need to change. Sometimes I envied how little effort boys had to put in to look good. Glob of hair gel, spritz of Lynx, and they were good to go.

I linked my arm through his as we headed for the stairs leading out of the flats. It was at the back of the building, but we preferred using it because it was typically empty. At the front of the flats you were guaranteed to run into arseholes looking for trouble.

We were almost to the end of the stairs when I saw a small group sitting on the bottom two steps. As we came closer, I recognised Dylan and his friends, Amy and Conor. They were a ragtag bunch, with Amy who did her best impression of Robert Smith from The Cure, and Conor, with his thick glasses and shaggy haircut. He was also mixed race, the only kid in the entire building with a white mother and an African father. Needless to say, things hadn't been easy for him.

Then there was Dylan, who was good-looking and smart enough to be friends with whoever he wanted. Instead he chose the most unlikely pair of besties. Maybe that's where the smart bit came in. Maybe he saw something the rest of us didn't.

It was one of the things I admired about him. He didn't conform, didn't follow the pack.

Normally, Sam and I might've walked by these three without so much as a hello, but since I now sort of knew Dylan, we stopped to greet them.

"Hey Dylan," said Sam. "You're looking a little better. Those bruises are healing up nicely."

I closed my eyes and grimaced. I mean, I loved Sam and all, but instead of avoiding elephants in rooms he tended to grab them by the tusks.

"What business is it of yours?" Amy asked defensively. Of all the girls who lived around here, she was definitely the prickliest. Then again, her taste in fashion tended to get a lot of negative attention, so maybe she had to be prickly. I often wondered why she did it. St Mary's Villas wasn't exactly the most welcoming to the goth of the species. Or to anyone who was different in any way for that matter.

I had to give her props for sticking to her guns.

She also constantly carried around this little video camera, recording random stuff throughout the day. I think she was just obsessed with film and wanted to be, like, a director or something. Still, freaked people out when they spotted her recording them.

"I was just saying," Sam replied. "No need to bite my head off."

Amy narrowed her eyes at him and took a swig of the can of lager she was holding. There was a six-pack next to Dylan, which told me how the three planned to spend their night. They certainly weren't heading to the disco.

Dylan's attention came to me, starting at my boots and then making a slow ascent up my body. The way he looked at me so thoroughly gave me butterflies, a very rare and specific type. Dylan O'Dea butterflies were the kind people trapped and displayed in picture frames.

My awareness of him was weird, because up until now I'd never really paid him much attention, other than absentmindedly noting he was attractive and tended to avoid the usual cliques at school.

Maybe I should let strange boys burst into my flat more often.

"Where are you off to?" he asked in that low voice of his.

"The disco over at Sweeney's," I answered and tugged my jacket tighter around me.

He never broke eye contact when he asked, "Why?"

I frowned. "What do you mean why?"

"Ev loves to dance," Sam put in. "That's why we're going."

Amy let out a quiet scoff, and I bristled but didn't say anything. Conor shyly stared at the ground, and Dylan continued to watch me.

I held up a hand and added, "Guilty as charged."
Man, why did I say that?

Before I had time to feel embarrassed, Dylan reached out, grabbed said hand, and pulled me down to sit next to him. A rush of breath escaped me at how familiarly he touched me.

"Stay and have a drink with us instead. Consider this the favour I owe you."

"How is that a favour?" I asked.

"Because it'll save you spending a single second dancing to 90s pop and getting come-ons from drunk fifteen-year-olds."

"Ha! He's not wrong," Sam chirped, going to take a seat beside Amy, in spite of her hostile attitude. That was Sam for you. He wasn't put off by shade. Quite like the elephants, he stared it square in the eye and killed it with his sunshine.

I was still deciding whether I wanted to stay and hang out with Dylan instead of going to Sweeney's, when Shane Huntley and his group walked into the building. Shane had a shaved head and wore a perennial uniform of jeans, Ben Sherman shirts, and pristinely white Adidas runners. That was when he wasn't in some skewed version of our school uniform. Some days his tie would be around his head—Rambo style. Others he'd a have a shirt but no jumper, or a jumper with no shirt. He was either very bad at laundry, or simply refused to play by the rules.

He quickly took in our group, looking at Sam the longest. A strange, almost pained look passed his features before he covered it with a sneer. I didn't typically hate people, but I hated Shane for how he treated Sam.

"How's it going, lads?" he asked, pulling a cigarette from behind his ear to light up.

"I think you'll find there are females here, too," Amy bristled.

Shane looked from Amy and then to me when he replied, "I don't see any."

Oh, good one. I internally rolled my eyes.

His friends snickered, and I noticed Dylan stiffen beside me. Shane cast him a brief, assessing look before he focused his attention on Sam. At school, Sam was something of a target for Shane. It'd be a rare day he didn't throw some homophobic insult or other, and it seemed today was not rare.

"What are you doing here, Sammy? Shouldn't you be down The George tonight getting bummed in the toilets?"

The George was a well-known gay bar in town. I clenched my jaw, about to shoot off an angry retort when Sam got there first. "Why? You like thinking about that?"

Shane's features went from snickering to furious in an instant. "The fuck did you just say?"

At this, Dylan stood and took a step towards Shane. He folded his arms and stared him down. "It's time for you to go."

"I'm not scared of you, O'Dea. Heard the McCarthy lads kicked the shite outta ya the other day, and I see the rumours are true."

Dylan took his time picking up his can, downed the rest of the contents, then tossed it aside. "The rumours will be true about me shutting up that dumb mouth of yours."

Shane stared at him, all squinty eyed as though trying to figure out if he should keep pushing. "It'd take better men than you to shut me up," he finally replied before turning to his buddies. "Come on. Reeks of faggot around here."

One of his friends slid their snaky eyes to Conor, muttering something awful under their breath as they walked away. Amy clearly heard it, too, because she stood up next to Dylan, fuming.

"Wow, a homophobe and a racist. You lot deserve each other."

A couple of them gave her the finger as they threw more insults. She clenched her fists, and Conor reached out, telling her it wasn't worth it.

When they were gone, Dylan sat back down, but the rigid set of his posture said he was still seething. I didn't know Dylan well at all, but watching him stand up for Sam meant a lot to me. He barely knew us, yet he was quick to defend. I felt I should thank him somehow, but wasn't sure what to say.

"Anyone notice how he didn't deny the dumb part?" asked Conor, as though to break the tension.

I smiled at him. "I think being stupid is considered cool among his type."

"You're probably right. And they just keep having babies. Before we know it, the world will be like that movie, *Idiocracy*."

"And Shane will be president," I shuddered. "What a thought."

"Ah, but we can be the ones to start up the resistance," he countered. "We'll call ourselves the Anti-Huntleys."

"Yeah, you two can be the Brad and Angelina of the rebellion," Sam crooned as he winked at me. Jeez, ever since Brad's divorce from Jennifer Aniston last year, Sam had been obsessed with his new relationship with Angelina Jolie. He always managed a way to work them into a conversation. And I knew his wink indicated he thought I was flirting with Conor, which I absolutely was not.

Conor blushed and looked away as Dylan cracked open a lager. He silently handed it to me, before grabbing another for Sam. I uttered a quiet "thanks" and took a sip.

"Evelyn's not the one Conor's interested in. He likes them older," Amy revealed, and Conor shot her a murderous look.

"Shut the fuck up, Amy," he whispered stiffly.

"Well now, what's all this about?" Sam enquired.

"He's into the aunt," said Amy, not caring that Conor shot her daggers with his eyes.

I turned to gape at him. "You like Yvonne?"

He shrugged, embarrassed. "She's nice to me."

Yvonne was nice to everyone. She had a heart as big as all outdoors, and Conor lived just a few flats down from ours. He must've bumped into her from time to time. Although I was pretty sure Yvonne didn't see him the same way. And that was before you even factored in the age gap.

"How old are you?"

"Eighteen," he replied, defensive.

"Well, my aunt's twenty-seven. That's a nine-year age difference."

"If it were the other way around, nobody would bat an eye," Dylan said. His voice licked at my senses. He'd been quiet since Shane left. I cast him a quick glance and saw he was studying my profile. I looked away again.

"Exactly," Amy put in. "There's nothing wrong with an age gap, so long as both parties are legal and consenting."

"I never said there was. I'm just pretty sure my aunt wouldn't see it that way. Any boyfriends she's had have been older."

"That makes no matter," said Sam. "I think you should tell her, Conor. Lay your feelings all out on the table with some big romantic gesture."

Conor grimaced while I reached out to give Sam a light slap. "Don't be an arse."

If Conor did that, he'd only embarrass himself, and Sam knew it. He was trying to stir up mischief. I looked to Conor, took in his messy, shaggy haircut, bottle-end glasses and skinny frame. He wasn't ugly, in fact, he had a kind, pleasant face, but he was so teenage it was painful. And he didn't look eighteen. He looked fifteen, sixteen at a push. Yvonne probably thought of him as another random kid who lived in the flats.

"Maybe wait a year or two," I told him kindly. "Then you'll be twenty, and it won't matter so much."

He let out a beleaguered sigh. "God, it's not like I'm in love with her or anything. I just think she's pretty. And she always wears high heels."

"Oh, you like that, do ya?" asked Sam with a wink.

"Most men do," Dylan spoke quietly. The way he said it sent pinpricks down my spine.

"I prefer a nice pair of Levis and a tight crotch myself," Sam replied, and Dylan's lips twitched ever so slightly.

"Oh yeah?"

"Yeah. You should get yourself a pair. I'm sure Ev wouldn't mind."

Oh, Sam, shut up now, please.

Dylan gently nudged me in the shoulder. "Is that so?"

"Don't listen to him," I mumbled under my breath, blushing like mental. Sam was *so* going to get it later.

"Shane Huntley wears Levis," Amy said, eyeing Sam shrewdly. "Is that where your preference stems from?" I was thankful to her for taking the spotlight off me and putting it on Sam. Little shit deserved it.

Like always though, he took it in stride, avoiding the question with perfect deflection. "Speaking of Shane, Ev has a theory. She thinks his bullying is a result of repressed homosexuality. Apparently, it's Freudian."

I was surprised he'd actually been listening. "It's just something I read. It might not be true."

"No, you have a point," said Dylan, and his validation sent a rush of pleasure through me. "I read an article once about a study carried out on a group of

29

men, and the ones who displayed the most homophobic views had higher levels of genital vascularity when shown images of male-on-male intimacy."

Sam widened his eyes at me before he addressed Dylan. "I can't say I've ever heard anyone use the phrase 'genital vascularity' in polite company before."

I chuckled. "But you hear it in impolite company?"

He waved me off. "You know what I mean."

"You've been reading too many of Yvonne's historical romance novels."

"Yvonne reads romance novels?" Conor leapt on that bit of info.

I glanced at him. "Yes, she does. A lot of women do."

He looked down as he went on. "Are they, uh, the sexy kind?"

"Oh man, you've got it bad. I'm not telling you that. I don't like the idea of you fantasising about my aunt."

"Too late for that." Dylan chuckled before he knocked back a gulp of lager. I glanced at him. He really was a dark horse. Reading studies about bias and human sexuality certainly wasn't something I'd expect of a teenage boy from St Mary's Villas. I mean, I only knew about that sort of stuff because Yvonne was such a broad reader. She'd never had the money to go to college, but she'd always cultivated her learning in her spare time. As a result, I tended to absorb some second-hand knowledge, since I was usually the one around for her to bounce ideas off.

"Shut it," Conor whispered, embarrassed again.

"There's nothing to be shy about," said Sam. "Yvonne's one hot mama. If I was straight I'd be fantasising about her, too."

"But instead you fantasise about Shane," Amy countered.

"Oh my God, will you stop? Despite Ev's and Dylan's fancy ideas, he's not gay. He's just a bully."

"Yeah, a sexy bully that you like to daydream about," she continued to goad.

I decided to help out my friend, even though he hadn't earned it. "Nah, Sam's too busy daydreaming about Jared Leto. There's no room for anyone else."

Amy's eyebrows shot up as she looked to Sam. "Wow, there's one thing you actually have good taste in."

"Hands off Mr Leto," said Sam, back to playful. "He's all mine."

"Have any of you seen this?" Conor interrupted, hitting play on a video on his phone, which looked to be top of the line. He ought not to be flashing that around the Villas or someone might steal it. The video showed a compilation of an Asian guy jumping from various rooftops, railings, and walls.

"Better him than me," said Sam. "That's impressive though."

"I know. Everyone's going wild for it online," said Conor. "It's some mean party trick."

"It's actually called free running," said Dylan. "And it's a sport, not a party trick."

"You're a party trick snob," said Amy. "You think you have the best one."

"What can you do?" I asked.

"He can identify any smell," Conor explained, like it was the most amazing thing ever.

"You lot are easily impressed," Sam commented dryly. "I'm pretty sure most people can do that."

"No, you don't understand. Dylan can smell any one thing and tell you all the ingredients, from a pasta sauce to a scented candle. It's crazy," Conor went on.

Dylan looked at me as he spoke. "My mam was born with a diminished sense of smell, so from when I was young she always had me describe what things smelled like. Over time I got used to picking out scents and breaking them down into their various components. I mean, I might not get every single one, especially if it's chemical based. But natural ingredients I can usually pick out."

"So, kind of like how seasoned musicians can listen to Beethoven and pick out all the instruments," I ventured and his eyes crinkled in a smile.

"Yes, like that."

"I can't believe your mam can't smell. How does she know when to wash, or if there's like, a gas leak in the flat?" Sam asked, and I stiffened at his question.

I knew Dylan's mother had passed away. I remembered seeing him and his dad leave for the funeral, all sad shoulders, black clothes. I stood on the balcony, watching them both down below. His dad threw his arm around his son and helped him into the waiting car, their lives forever changed . . .

I blinked myself out of the memory. It was about three years ago, which was probably why Sam didn't remember. I knew she died of cancer, having heard the gossip around the flats, but I didn't know the specifics.

"Actually, she's passed," Dylan explained, lips dipping downward. "So those things don't really matter anymore."

For a brief second, he looked like he'd give anything to have those trivialities back again, to have his mam back.

"Oh, my goodness, I'm so sorry," Sam exclaimed, looking guilty. "I didn't know."

"No worries. It was a couple of years ago," said Dylan, and a moment of awkward silence fell. I thought a subject change was in order.

"So, can we put your talent to the test? I want to see it in action."

Dylan's attention came to me. "Sure, give me anything, and I'll tell you what's in it."

"How about this booze?" said Sam, thrusting his can at him. Dylan took it and brought it to his nose, inhaling deeply.

"So, the rest of you probably wouldn't pick this up, but to me Heineken smells a lot like weed."

Sam made a face. "Weed? Seriously?"

Dylan nodded. "The hops they use are closely related to cannabis, because they both come from the Cannabaceae plant family. Also, you probably gave me too much of an easy one. Most people know Heineken has only three ingredients: water, malted barley, and hops."

Cannabaceae plant family? Now he was talking my language. Seriously, how had I never noticed how interesting Dylan O'Dea was before?

"Well, dammit," Sam sighed, "I don't have anything else."

"Hold on, I might," I said and rummaged in my bag to pull out a pot of lip balm. Yvonne got it for me from an organic cosmetics place, so I knew it was all-natural ingredients. If you peeled the sticker away at the back there was a list, but I hid that from Dylan's view. "Try this," I went on and handed him the pot.

He screwed off the lid and took a sniff. The way he smelled things was weirdly attractive. He gave it his entire focused attention, inhaling deeply, like it was a fine wine or a rare flower. "Hmm, so the top notes are mostly nutty, but I can also get a strong scent of coconut and chocolate, with a hint of vanilla. The base note is Shea butter," he finished, handing it back to me with confidence.

I took the pot and read the ingredients on the back, astounded to find he'd named almost all of them.

"That's insane," said Sam, swiping the pot from me to smell it himself. "All I can get is chocolate."

"Smell is like any other sense. Like Evelyn said, where we hear a complete piece of music, a trained musician can pick out every instrument. You can train your nose to do exactly the same thing, it just takes time."

"But why would you want to do that?" Sam asked, curious.

Dylan shrugged. "That I can't tell you. It's just something I've always been interested in."

"That's like Ev and her plants. She's obsessed."

"Oh right, don't you have that little garden on the roof?" Amy asked. "I've seen you up there once or twice."

"Yes, I got permission from the local council to start an allotment. Not many people around here are interested though," I replied.

"I didn't know that," Dylan said, a frown marring his features. It was almost like he thought he knew everything about me and was confused by this new piece of info. But that was ridiculous. We only spoke for the first time a few days ago. He didn't know me at all.

I bobbed my head. "It's true. So far, it's just me, Mrs O'Flaherty from the top floor and her grandson, Seamus. But I'm optimistic I can get more people into gardening over time. My newest obsession is succulent plants, like aloe vera and cacti. I've been driving Yvonne crazy by filling up the flat with them, but they make the place feel so much more cheerful. And they take hardly any watering. All you do is soak the soil until it turns really dark and wet, then you don't water them again until it dries out, which usually takes about a week."

I realised I was babbling and shut up. Very few people got as excited about gardening as I did.

"You see," said Sam. "She practically turns herself on talking about it."

Dylan ignored him, his attention still on me, and I liked how he seemed interested instead of bored. "What have you planted on the roof?"

"Oh, a whole bunch of stuff. Some of my wildflowers are in bloom at the moment, and the bees just love them. When it's sunny, there's a constant stream of buzzy customers coming to collect the pollen. It's so fascinating."

"You must be easily entertained," Amy commented, but I wasn't bothered by her cynicism. I was used to people finding my hobby uninteresting. I looked back to Dylan, surprised when I noted that his handsome features still showed interest. It gave me the courage to continue.

"My big dream is actually to start beekeeping on the roof. Did you know we're slowly running out of bees?"

"Wouldn't that be a good thing?" Amy asked, and I got the sense that she didn't like me, or at best, found me dull. "All they do is sting people. I once heard about a girl from Crumlin who died from an allergic reaction to a bee sting."

"Honeybees only sting to protect their hive," I said, defending my little winged friends. "Bees out in the wild collecting pollen rarely sting. They do it if they think you're a threat, and they usually die afterwards, so you know, it's not like they go around actively looking to hurt people."

"Yeah well, I wouldn't mind a world without honey if it meant we didn't have bees buzzing around stinging people because they feel threatened," she huffed.

Dylan frowned at her. "If we didn't have bees, humans would die out."

She scoffed at this. "No, we wouldn't."

He exhaled a breath, as though frustrated. "We need bees for pollination, otherwise half the food we eat wouldn't grow. And they're dying out because of the pesticides we use in modern farming." He paused to look at me again. "I think it's a great idea to start beekeeping on the roof. It's not like the space is being used for anything else."

Oh Dylan, stop being so clever and nice or I'll develop a crush.

"That's our Ev for ya," said Sam. "Trying to save the human race."

"The human race is hardly so great," Amy grumped.

She looked embarrassed, and though it could be due to Dylan's reprimand about the importance of bees, I wondered if she felt a little threatened by me. After all, just like Sam was my people, Dylan and Connor were hers. Maybe she saw me as an interloper.

"Well, you have a point there," I said, hoping to assuage her. I didn't want her to dislike me. It was one of my biggest shortcomings; I always wanted people to like me, and sometimes they weren't worth the effort. Though I suspected underneath all her make-up and snark, Amy was a sweet girl.

There was a moment of quiet as we took a sip of our drinks. Then Conor asked, "Does Yvonne help out with your allotment?"

Ha! Yeah right, he wasn't in love with her. At the very least he was thoroughly besotted.

"If I say yes, does that mean you'll come and start your own patch?" I asked, hopeful. I wasn't above telling a little white lie to get more participants. Yeah, I was that desperate.

He fiddled with the leg of his glasses. "Maybe."

I sighed. "She doesn't *exactly* take part, but she does pop up to say hello every now and again. If you start a plot, there's a chance you'll bump into her."

"Or he could just go get a pint down at The Morgan and try chatting her up," Sam suggested.

I reached out to slap his shoulder. "Shut it. I almost had him. You know how much I need more people, especially since you can't be relied upon to make up the numbers."

"Ev, you start at six in the morning sometimes. Do you know how godawful early that is? No wonder so few people are interested."

"I'm interested," Dylan blurted, surprising me. My cheeks flushed as I glanced at him.

"Really? You're not put off by the early start? If you are, you can come on the weekend. I don't usually get up there until around ten on a Sunday."

He lifted the can to his mouth, smiling around a long gulp of lager. "I'll drop by when I can."

"Great, yeah. I'm there most mornings," I said, pleased, ignoring Sam as he waggled his brows from behind Dylan.

It seemed the old adage was true.

Go out for a disco, and find a new gardening recruit instead.

Three

I was walking by the chemistry labs on my way to lunch the next time I saw Dylan. He had a white coat on and was huddled over what appeared to be an experiment. The teacher was focused on marking papers and eating lunch at the front of the classroom.

Dylan was a year ahead of me, studying for his Leaving Certificate. I wondered if he planned to go to college when he finished or if he'd just get a job. I mean, college must've been on his radar, especially if he was spending his lunch hour working on an experiment instead of eating in the cafeteria with his friends.

There were two other students in the classroom, but both were focused on their own work. Higher-level chemistry wasn't a subject a lot of kids took at this school. After third year, most moved down a level, or dropped out completely, so there were typically only five or six students total in those classes.

I'd chosen biology as my science subject, because I didn't have a head for chemistry or physics, but I was willing to bet Dylan was one of those rare breeds who took all three. He struck me as the type.

While I studied him he glanced up, like he sensed my attention. I jumped and his brows furrowed, but I saw him start to smile when I looked away and hurried down the corridor, embarrassed he caught me watching.

Sam had choir practice on Mondays, so I headed home on my own at the end of the day. I was almost to the school gates when a voice called, "Evelyn, hold up."

Dylan jogged casually towards me, backpack over one shoulder. It looked heavy, stuffed full of books.

He was a tiny bit out of breath when he caught up to me, although that was probably more from the weight of the bag than the run. "Can I walk with you?"

I opened my mouth to respond, but there was a delay to my words. Kind of like on TV when a newsreader was speaking to a field reporter via satellite. I was just a little stunned that this older, attractive, smart and interesting boy had run up to me. Was seemingly going out of his way to be *friends* with me. It wasn't something that happened often. Or ever. I wasn't one of the cool, pretty girls at school who boys chased after. Don't get me wrong, like Yvonne and my mam, I *was* pretty, but most people considered me too flighty, too much in my own little world to bother pursuing.

Hence, at seventeen, I was still a virgin.

And yes, I know that wasn't exactly old-maid status, but at St Mary's Villas most girls fell pregnant and dropped out of school by sixteen. In fact, my mam was fifteen when she had me.

I looked at Dylan, finally managing to get some words out. Well, one word. "Sure."

"I saw you earlier," he said, and my previous embarrassment rushed back.

"Right, yeah, I was, uh, on my way to lunch. You looked dead focused. I don't think I've ever been that concentrated at school. I'm too easily distracted."

"I was working on an experiment extracting iodine from seaweed. Was I pulling a weird face or something?" he asked with a chuckle.

"Nah, your eyebrows were just all furrowed. How did your experiment go?"

"Good. Mr Tully allows some of us work through our lunch hour when he eats at his desk. That way he can keep an eye on us in case we set ourselves on fire."

"Has that actually happened?" I asked with a nervous laugh.

Dylan shook his head. "Not as far as I know, but I needed to heat the seaweed to extract the iodine, and Mr Tully would've chewed me out if I did it without supervision."

"But he wasn't watching you at all. He was just sitting there. If you made a mistake you could've lost your eyebrows," I replied, teasing.

Dylan laughed. "At least I could start a new fashion trend."

"Nope, it'd never take. Everyone looks better with eyebrows."

"Coming from the girl who barely has any," Dylan shot back with a grin.

"Hey. I have eyebrows. They're just very blonde."

"Well, no one would ever suspect you dye your hair."

"Yep. When I was little it was white. I looked like one of those Children of the Corn."

Dylan hitched his bag higher on his shoulder and studied my profile for a second. "I don't believe you. You smile too much to ever be a creepy corn child."

I self-consciously tucked some hair behind my ear. "I do?"

He nodded. "It's the reason I knocked on your door the other day. I thought, someone who smiles as much as you do has to be a Good Samaritan."

"Not necessarily. It could be a sinister smile. I could be secretly plotting everyone's demise behind it."

"Ah well, fortunately for me, I can tell the difference."

We walked in silence for a minute, and my mind raced, thinking of him noticing me before I ever really noticed him. Butterflies. I had butterflies again.

I mean, he must've noticed me a lot if he knew I smiled all the time. *And knew where I lived.* Funnily enough, I wasn't at all creeped out by that. Instead, a thrilling rush went through me. Dylan was too warm, felt too authentic to ever be a creep. I wanted to say something to him, prolong the conversation. I scrambled for an appropriate subject and the first thing that entered my head was his iodine experiment.

"I used to always think all those science experiments were so impractical, but maybe not. Remember after 9/11, when the government sent a box of iodine tablets to every house in the country in case Sellafield got bombed? If that ever happened, you could earn a mint manufacturing iodine, using the same method."

I half expected Dylan to be like, *what are you rambling about?* But he didn't miss a beat when he chuckled. "You could be on to something. My dad said they didn't send enough for everyone in the household, and the tablets were almost out of date."

"What a joke. The nuclear power plant would be attacked, and we'd all be dead from radiation."

"Yep. And the east coast would be the worst hit if that ever happened. So, you and I would be pretty much screwed."

"Better live life to the fullest while we can then," I said, jokingly.

"It wouldn't even need to be a terrorist attack, you know," Dylan continued, like he was suddenly on a roll. "There's already a huge nuclear dump just a hundred and sixty kilometres off our coast. If it ever leaks, and there's a good chance it will, we'll all be living in a Chernobyl-like situation."

"Wow, you really know how to cheer a girl up," I replied, though I was impressed he knew all this. Plus, I had been the one to bring up the topic.

His mouth dipped at the edges as he scratched his jaw. "Sorry. I have a problem with fixating on negative stuff sometimes. My dad is the exact same. You wouldn't want to live at our house. Like Dad says, the sky is always falling for the O'Dea men."

"I'm sure you're not that bad."

"Want to bet? Just wait until I get started on global warming and how it's going to set civilised society back to barbarian times. You'll be slitting your wrists within the hour," he quipped, but there was an odd note of truth to his words.

"Well, Amy and Conor haven't resorted to suicide, and they're your best friends," I countered.

"That's because Amy's a goth. She loves doom and gloom. And Conor's known me so long he's desensitised. Why do you think I can't get a girlfriend? I depress every girl I meet."

I found that very hard to believe. Besides, it wasn't true. I heard the talk around the school. I knew there were plenty of girls who fancied Dylan, but thought he was too preoccupied and aloof. I was pretty sure most people didn't know how to broach a conversation with him. And when they did they were probably intimidated by his imposing form and intelligence and gave up.

"I don't find you depressing. I find you interesting. Plus, you don't fall asleep when I talk about my allotment, so you get points for that."

He nudged me with his shoulder. "Want to be my girlfriend then?"

My heart skipped a beat, but I didn't let it show. "Funny," I deadpanned, while on the inside I hesitated. Was he being serious? Nah, he had to be kidding.

Despite the quiet between us, it didn't feel uncomfortable, which surprised me. We ascended the steps when we reached the Villas. Since Dylan lived a few floors below me, we arrived at his flat first.

"Well, I guess I'll see you at school," I said, glancing at him. "Unless you want to invite me in?"

It wasn't like me to be so forward, but I didn't want to say goodbye yet. Hanging out with him and talking felt oddly exhilarating. We weren't doing anything exciting, just walking home from school, but still, my pulse sped like we were riding a rollercoaster.

Weird.

"My dad's inside," he said, a bit uncomfortable. "So, it's probably best if you don't."

I furrowed my brow. "Why?"

Dylan rubbed his neck, obviously torn. "He's, um, kind of eccentric."

"I like eccentric," I replied, though I thought Dylan was exaggerating. I'd seen his dad around from time to time, and he looked pretty normal to me. Nothing weird or unusual about him.

The tiniest hint of resignation claimed his features. "Okay well, let's see if you still feel that way after you meet him."

He slotted his key in the door and stepped inside. I followed, finding a neat but very overstuffed living space. Shelves packed with books lined the walls, newspapers and magazines were stacked high on the coffee table, and there was a tower of plastic storage boxes full of miscellaneous stuff beside the couch. Dylan's dad sat on an armchair by the TV watching one of the news stations.

"Have you seen the latest story about MRSA?" he asked when he heard us come in, not turning his attention from the screen. "They're now saying it can be spread from ordinary objects in the hospital, like folders and pens. The organism can stick to things and live for up to eighty days. I think I might need to cancel my check-up next week. With my compromised immunity, I'd die if I caught the bug."

"You don't have a compromised immunity, Dad. You're just run-down because you don't sleep enough,"

Dylan replied, setting his bag on the floor as he walked over to open the window.

"I had a throbbing pain in my neck this morning and my glands are swollen. It could be leukaemia," his Dad went on, totally serious.

Dylan took a second to rub his temple then knelt in front of his dad and reached out to feel both sides of his neck and under his jaw. "Your glands feel fine to me. Like I said, you just need to sleep. And you're not cancelling your check-up. You need your prescription refilled anyway."

His dad tutted and turned his head, finally seeing me. His cheeks reddened, and he appeared embarrassed he didn't notice me sooner. "Dylan, you should've told me you brought a friend over. Hello, I'm Tommy," he said, standing and coming to shake my hand. I was surprised by the welcome.

"I'm Evelyn. I live upstairs," I replied and shook with him. "It's nice to meet you."

"And you, Evelyn. I recognise your face. Aren't you Yvonne Flynn's young one?"

"No, I'm her niece. Lily's my mam, but I live with Yvonne now."

"Right, yes," said Tommy, smacking his forehead like he should've known. "Well, come in and sit down. Dylan rarely brings friends over. The only ones I ever see are Conor and that Amy girl."

I sat on the small couch, sliding my bag off my shoulder and onto the floor. Dylan's dad studied me a moment, like something just occurred to him.

"My goodness, do you know what? I think I was the one who drove your mother to the hospital when she went into labour," he exclaimed. "I used to drive a taxi, but I gave that up a few years back. It's too dangerous nowadays. Any kind of nutcase could climb into the back of my car."

"There's always been nutcases, Dad. It's hardly a new thing," Dylan said, his posture tense, eyes flicking between his dad and me like he was waiting for judgement. I, on the other hand, was far too preoccupied with what he said about my mam. "You drove my mam to the hospital?"

I knew very little about my birth, mostly because Mam didn't talk about stuff like that. All I knew was she got pregnant from having sex with some random boy when she'd barely turned fifteen.

"Yes, your aunt and granny weren't around, so she called for a taxi to take her to the Rotunda. Poor thing was terrified. I called my Maureen, God rest her soul, to come and help calm her down on the drive. She left Dylan at the neighbour's and stayed with your mam throughout her labour, only leaving when your aunt and granny showed up."

Wow. I couldn't believe I'd never heard this before. Maureen, Dylan's mam, must've been a nice lady to stay and comfort a young pregnant teen while she gave birth. Was that why I felt a connection to Dylan? Or was it simply because he was so different from other boys, an enigma?

"I never knew that," I breathed, emotion fisting my heart. I'd always been so dismissive of Mam and her

48

selfish decision to leave, but maybe I needed to think of things from her perspective. She was two years younger than I am now when she had me. With no job or education, no prospects, she must've been terrified. I made a mental note to ask Gran some more about the pregnancy the next time I visited her at the home.

"Well, some people don't like to talk about these things," said Tommy, a touch of sympathy to his voice. "When Maureen went into labour with Dylan, I wanted to vomit I was so nervous. Childbirth can be a terrifying thing. In my mother's day, most women suffered several miscarriages, or even stillbirths over the course of their lives. It was just the way of things, what with there being such poor healthcare and a lack of contraception. We can thank the Catholic church for that," he added with a hint of derision.

"Dad," Dylan said, a warning. I thought he might be worried I'd be offended.

"What? I'm sure Evelyn is aware of the church's history in this country, swiping babies from young mothers and selling them off to the highest bidder. It was disgraceful the way some of those nuns treated the women in their care. I mean, they were more or less imprisoned for the simple act of having a child out of wedlock. Lily Flynn was lucky she didn't fall into the same trap with young Evelyn here. The Magdalene laundries were still active up until the mid-nineties, you know."

"Dad, please," Dylan gritted, but Tommy just kept going.

"And do you know why they were named after Mary Magdalene?" he scoffed. "Because she was a reformed prostitute. As though falling pregnant at a young age is akin to prostitution. And of course, *that's* what they were doing, reforming these girls, not stealing their babies to make a quick buck and getting free labour in the process."

"*Okay*," Dylan announced, standing abruptly. He came and took my hand in his, and the familiar touch surprised me. "We're going to my room to do homework." I grabbed my bag before I was dragged away.

"Right, sure, I'll make dinner in a bit," his dad replied, like there was nothing wrong. And there wasn't. However, it did make me feel vaguely ill to think of some alternate reality where my mam was sent to a workhouse. I let Dylan lead me down the hallway.

His room was tiny, and like the rest of the flat there was very little space. He had a single bed against the wall, a small window, some shelves, and a wardrobe. "I like your dad," I said as I sat down on his bed. It felt weirdly intimate, but there was literally nowhere else to sit. "Really, I do. You don't need to worry about him offending me or anything."

Dylan exhaled a breath as he grabbed some textbooks from the shelf. "You don't have to pretend. I know he's not exactly normal."

"Who's normal? We all have little eccentricities in the privacy of our own homes."

"Right, I'm sure you're such a freak," Dylan huffed grumpily. I couldn't believe he was being so crabby about this. We all got a little embarrassed by our family members every once in a while. It was a part of life.

"I was just saying, there's no need to be annoyed at your dad. He's interesting."

"Glad you enjoyed the freak show," he replied scornfully.

"Dylan," I said, my voice firm.

He glanced at me, face hard. "What?"

"You're being an arsehole, so I think I'm going to leave now."

I stood and grabbed my bag, throwing it over my shoulder. Dylan's expression hardened further, a conflict in his gaze. However, the stubborn set of his jaw told me he wasn't someone who backed down in arguments very often.

"Go then," he grumped and focused his attention on flicking through his textbook.

I narrowed my gaze, turned on my heel and went. Even though he'd been feigning preoccupation with the book, I sensed him watch me leave. Not long ago, I hadn't really known who Dylan O'Dea was. In my flat, he'd been careful, strong, protective. In the stairwell, he'd been engaging, gallant, and astute. Now? Now he was being childish and difficult. *Which was kinda funny, really.* He rarely brought people over, yet he brought me inside his home only to turn around and act like an arse.

All I knew was, if he wanted to continue being friends, he better be the one to apologise.

Four

It was one of those mild, sunny September mornings. My favourite. I loved autumn most of all, because even though the leaves fell from the trees, their pretty colours lit up the streets surrounding the Villas. They covered all the depressing grey concrete with browns and yellows and dusky reds.

Mrs O'Flaherty and Seamus were already on the roof when I arrived at my allotment. Mrs O'Flaherty favoured growing vegetables, while I was much more interested in flowers. In fact, my echinacea were currently in full bloom, the purple petals standing to attention under the morning sun.

I planned to clip them today and take some to my gran when I visited her at the home this evening. Grandma Flynn was the one who first introduced me to gardening, and though she was too infirm to garden herself, she loved it when I brought her the flowers I'd grown.

"Morning, Seamus, morning, Mrs O'Flaherty," I greeted as I went to ready my tools and put on my gardening gloves.

"Good morning, Evelyn," Mrs O'Flaherty replied, while Seamus shyly bobbed his head. He wasn't much of a talker, more of a silent, watchful type, with perennially rosy cheeks. He was about my age, and he attended an all-boys school, which probably explained his inability to talk to me. He wasn't used to being around girls.

"Those cherry tomatoes are looking good," I commented, and Mrs O'Flaherty seemed pleased with the compliment.

"I'm very happy with how they turned out, though most of the praise should go to Seamus. He did the lion's share of the work."

I glanced at Seamus and smiled. "Well done, we'll make a farmer out of you yet."

"Fat chance of that," Mrs O'Flaherty scoffed. "My son's having him take law at Trinity next year."

"If I manage to get in," Seamus added quietly.

"Trinity, eh?" I commented. "Fancy."

"There are grants I can apply for," he explained, as though worried I'd presume he was rich or something. He might not have lived in the flats, but his grandma liked to talk, so I knew he wasn't wealthy. His dad was an English teacher and his mam a special needs care worker.

"Oh, right," I said. I had no intention of applying to college myself. I wanted to get a job, like Yvonne, and pay my way. If I could get work on a flower farm, it'd be ideal.

"I'm thinking of growing some rhubarb this year," Mrs O'Flaherty went on, and I grimaced. I hated rhubarb, not just as a vegetable, but as a plant, too. It was an invasive species, and once grown, had a habit of spreading like wildfire, leaving no room for anything else. We'd once gone on a school trip to Achill Island, and the place was literally overrun with the stuff.

"Well, just make sure you keep it to one section of the allotment. I don't want to deal with an invasion."

"I love a bit of rhubarb crumble in the autumn," Mrs O'Flaherty said, wistfully.

I didn't comment because I honestly thought it was unpalatable. You had to use so much sugar to make it taste nice. You might as well eat a flipping strawberry instead.

"Need any help?" came a familiar voice, and I glanced up.

Dylan stood a few feet away, dressed casually in jeans and a T-shirt. The golden tones in his hair twinkled under the sun. I was more than a little surprised to see him, especially considering it had been a week since I'd stormed out of his flat. We hadn't talked at all since then, so his appearance made me feel a touch awkward. I was also miffed that Conor never bothered to show, even with the prospect of bumping into Yvonne to lure him.

"Uh, yes, sure. Let me go grab you a pair of gloves," I replied casually. I wouldn't let him know that each day he didn't try to make amends burned a new hole in my chest. It was unnerving how much I thought about him, given how little time we'd been acquainted.

"You're Tommy O'Dea's young lad, aren't you?" Mrs O'Flaherty asked, glancing at Dylan from under her sun hat.

"That's right," Dylan replied.

"How is he these days? Still not gone back to driving his taxi yet?"

"No, not yet." Dylan's posture stiffened.

"Oh, well, I'm sorry to hear that. Some people just aren't great at sticking with jobs, but do give him my best," she went on, a touch of haughtiness to her tone.

"I will." Dylan spoke quietly, firmly.

I cut Mrs O'Flaherty a sharp look, mostly because I took issue with people who hadn't worked a day in their lives condescendingly asking after other people's employment status. She had one son, Seamus's father, and she'd been a lady of leisure ever since he fled the nest a good twenty-five years ago, living off her late husband's pension. Also, because she talked so much, I knew her other grandson, Seamus's brother, was a twenty-three-year-old layabout with a bad marijuana habit, who spent most of his time in his bedroom playing the drums.

"Speaking of which," I said to Seamus, "how's your brother doing?"

Mrs O'Flaherty visibly stilled, her lips flattening into a thin line of displeasure as she dug her trowel into some soil.

Seamus let out a heavy sigh. "Still smoking weed. Still as lazy as ever."

I eyed Mrs O' Flaherty pointedly in quiet defence of Dylan, letting her know he wasn't the only one with weak spots. I wasn't sure why I did it, because it wasn't like Dylan and I were buddies. In fact, I wasn't sure if we were on speaking terms yet. I just didn't like people looking down on others, no matter the situation. I guess I knew what it felt like. Gossip abounded after Mam left me with Yvonne so she could swan off to London.

I walked to the other end of the allotment, and Dylan followed behind.

"Sorry about her," I said once we were out of earshot. "She can be a bit of a snob sometimes."

Dylan shrugged. "No worries."

"Though why anyone who lives in the Villas thinks they have a right to snobbery is beyond me," I went on, and Dylan showed the barest hint of a smile before clearing his throat.

"So, uh, I wanted to apologise for last week. You were right. I was an arsehole, and I'm sorry for that."

"Here, put these on. They might be a bit of a tight fit, but they're all I have right now," I said, uncomfortable with apologies.

Dylan appeared perplexed at my offering of girl-sized gloves. "That's okay. I'll bring my own next time. So, is my apology accepted or . . .?"

I shrugged. "You probably don't need them anyway. I'm clipping these echinacea flowers this morning. And yes, apology accepted."

"Good," Dylan murmured, his gaze sharpening on the small mole just under my jaw. "Because I've missed you."

A rush of air claimed my lungs at his statement. I tried to play it cool, while on the inside my heart raced. "You hardly know me."

"That's not true. I've known you for years."

I didn't know what to make of that, though in a way he was right. We'd been aware of each other's existence for years, but we'd never actually exchanged words. I eyed him for a second. "You're very honest."

"To a fault sometimes."

"I don't see how honesty can ever be a fault, not in the grand scheme of things."

"Oh, believe me, it can. Kind of like how I depress people with my doom and gloom, I also drive people away with my honesty. Most of us just want pleasant lies."

"Hmm," I said, pondering it. "You have a point. I'd much rather be told my arse looks good in jeans than fat."

Dylan absentmindedly took the clippers from me and carefully snipped a flower. "I never understood why women consider a fat arse a bad thing."

I grinned at that and Dylan brought the flower to his nose to breathe in. I'd almost forgotten about his preternatural sense of smell. "Sweet," he murmured, and I suppressed a swell of attraction at the way he inhaled so intently.

"Echinacea has a lot of medicinal properties. You can dry it and turn it into a tea, or you can simply eat them like this," I said, pulling off a petal and sticking it in my mouth. "Although, personally, I think the flowers are too pretty not to put in a vase and admire, at least for a little while."

Dylan watched me curiously while I chewed the petal, his eyebrows rising ever so slightly. "Has anyone ever told you you're a little odd?"

"This coming from the king of gloom."

"That must be why I don't scare you. Your oddness counteracts my gloominess."

"Speaking of odd, have you ever heard of miracle berries?"

Dylan let out a chuckle. "You see. You are odd, Evelyn Flynn. If I'm the king of gloom, you're the queen of randomness."

I smiled at that. He really was incredibly gorgeous, especially when he chuckled. *He said he'd missed me. Dylan O'Dea had missed me.* Berries. I was talking about berries.

"No seriously, I just read about them the other day. They're this small red fruit from Africa, and after you eat them they make sour foods taste sweet."

"So, I could eat a lemon and it'd taste like an orange?"

"Exactly. I've been dying to find some to see if they work, but I don't think you can buy them here."

Dylan chuckled again before he clipped a few more flowers. I admired the way the muscles in his arms moved as he did so.

"Other girls your age dream about getting the latest shade of lipstick, or tickets to a Justin Timberlake concert. You dream about finding miracle berries for sale at the local supermarket."

I gave him a light shove and defended, "I just want to get my hands on those elusive fruits, okay?" Dylan shook his head, and I bit my lip as I studied him. "By the way, how's your dad been?"

His brows started to furrow. "He's fine. Why?"

"I was just thinking about what he said about feeling unwell. You shouldn't be so dismissive. He could actually be sick, you know."

Dylan's expression turned weary. "He's not sick. Well, not physically anyway. My dad's got depression, it makes him sort of fixate on things."

"Oh," I said. "Sorry. I didn't know."

"Don't apologise. He's always been prone to bouts of sadness, but after Mam passed away it got worse. Like, if there are kids hanging around outside the flat, he'll immediately think they're up to no good, trying to rob the place or something. Give him a situation and he'll always think the worst."

"That must be hard to live with sometimes," I said, feeling sad for him. I couldn't imagine what it must be like to have your parent constantly worrying. Yvonne and I were pretty similar in the sense that we always tried to look on the bright side. It was why living together was so easy.

Dylan nodded and went quiet then, just looking at me. I tucked some hair behind my ear, self-conscious as I asked, "What?"

He made a low hum and his eyes traced my features. "Just mentally berating myself for not befriending you sooner."

His statement made my cheeks heat, and my chest fluttered at the way he looked at me, so focused, so sincere.

"Is that what you're doing? Befriending me?"

His expression turned thoughtful, those handsome brows of his drawing together. "I think so."

We worked in quiet for a minute as I let that sink in. I was incredibly flattered that he wanted to know me. It wasn't often that you met someone and just clicked with them like I had with Dylan. I was also relieved that he seemed to accept there was no judgement on my part regarding his dad. I had enjoyed meeting him, and even though I felt sad for them both in different ways, I was fairly certain Dylan hadn't felt as though I'd judged him. How could I? I knew what it was like to lose someone I loved. Or be abandoned. At least Dylan's mam hadn't left him by choice.

A pang of hurt seized me, but I tried to ignore it as I gathered some flowers in a bunch and asked, "I don't suppose you're going to the school dance tonight?"

Every year in late September, the school put on an informal dance for students. Dylan disliked discos, so he probably wouldn't be attending. Sam and I always went, even if it was only to sit in a corner and gossip about people while commenting on their fashion choices.

Dylan's expression turned frustrated. "Conor wants to go. He's sort of holding me and Amy to ransom over it."

"How so?" I asked, curious.

"We both owe him one, since he went to a My Chemical Romance concert with Amy last month, and he's tutoring me in French this year. It's my worst subject."

"So, he's cashing in on the debt. I like his style," I said, smiling. "I think it'd be good for you and Amy to socialise like normal teenagers. You stick to your little trio too much."

"Coming from the girl who's rarely away from her best friend's side," Dylan countered.

"That's different. Sam and I are soulmates. There's no hope tearing us apart."

He appeared amused by this. "Well, anyway, to answer your question. Yes, I'm going, though if I had my way there'd be several miles and a body of water between me and any variety of organised fun."

"Man, you really are a grump," I teased.

There was the barest flash of a twinkle in his eye. "The grumpiest."

We stared at each other, both smiling, and a warmth spread through my chest.

"Evelyn, could we get your help down here for a minute?" Mrs O'Flaherty called, interrupting our moment.

"Sure," I responded, then to Dylan, "be back in a second."

Five

"Get a load of what Jackie Harrison's wearing. She looks like a pink blancmange," Sam observed cattily.

"It's called a ra-ra skirt, and they're all the rage for your information."

"Come on, it's a glorified tutu, and we both know it."

I smirked. "Maybe."

"Hold the boat," Sam exclaimed, hand whipping out and landing flat against my sternum. A whoosh of air fled my lungs at the impact. "Do my eyes deceive me or did Dylan, Conor, and Amy just walk in?"

"Your eyes aren't deceiving you. That's definitely them."

"Well fuck me slowly with a chainsaw. In all these years, I've never once seen any of them attend a school function."

"Conor wanted to come. He blackmailed Dylan and Amy into it, apparently."

"Now it makes sense."

I was momentarily taken aback by how hot Dylan looked. Well, hotter than usual. His hair was styled, and he was wearing a fitted shirt with formal slacks. The outfit made him look older, a lot older, and it was doing all sorts of things to me.

Things, I tell you.

"Dylan looks sexy, Amy's got her camcorder glued to her face, and Conor looks nerdy. I guess, all is right with the world," said Sam and I shook my head at him as my eyes found Dylan's across the crowded assembly hall. For tonight it had been cleared out to form a dance floor, with chairs around the outskirts and a DJ on the stage. Right now, he was playing "Buttons" by Pussycat Dolls.

"Okay, I can't resist those Pussycats. Let's go dance," Sam declared, surprising the hell out of me. He never danced in public, and I meant *never*.

"Has hell frozen over?" I asked, and he rolled his eyes.

"Just shut up and dance with me."

On the other side of the room, Shane Huntley was surrounded by his gang of stupids. I called them that because anybody who looked up to someone with an IQ of less than ninety had to be dumb as fuck. There was a weird moment when his attention fixed on Sam, his eyes narrowing, while Sam straightened his posture and shot him a look that was pure defiance.

Okay.

My friend was taking a stand.

I wore a floral skater dress that went to mid-thigh, black tights and a pair of cheap cowboy boots. They were totally in fashion right now, but I couldn't afford the real leather ones. My hair hung long and wavy down my back as I moved to the beat. Sam gave it his all, pulling his best moves like he hadn't a care in the world. When the song changed to "My Humps" we got giddy and couldn't stop laughing. It was one of The Black Eyed Peas's newer singles, and Sam and I found it hilarious. In fact, we sang it to each other at random all the time.

Nobody really knew what a hump was.

I mean, they thought they did, but did they really?

It was a question for the ages.

As I danced, I noticed Dylan, Amy, and Conor sitting only a few yards away. Amy and Conor were talking, but Dylan was watching Sam and me.

And smiling.

His smile was the facial equivalent of a hot water bottle, or a cup of warm cocoa.

Heated yet affectionate.

I started to smile back, when suddenly we were crowded. Shane and his stupids had come to join us, but they weren't being friendly. Shane glared at Sam, getting in his space and saying something to him over the music. Sam's expression hardened as he shot off a reply I couldn't hear. When Shane grabbed Sam by his shirt, I intervened, taking hold of Shane's shoulder and pulling him away from my friend.

"Don't touch him," I yelled and Shane swung around, punching me right across the face. My vision went dark for a second, and when I opened my eyes Dylan was there. He punched Shane hard, then pushed him to the floor before Amy and Conor came and pulled him away.

"I'm gonna fuck you up, O'Dea," Shane shouted angrily, holding on to his jaw.

I realised Sam had his arms around me when he gasped, "Oh my goodness."

"You make a habit of hitting girls, you piece of shite?" Dylan fumed. Conor and Amy almost had him out the door, but he was doing his best to fight them off.

"I didn't know it was her," Shane retorted, while Sam hustled me to the exit as well. We definitely needed to get out of there before any teachers got involved. As soon as I stepped out the door, Dylan was on me. His hands cupped my face as he studied me for injuries. He looked frantic. Angry.

"I'll kill him," he breathed, then swore under his breath. "I'll fucking kill him."

"He didn't know it was Ev," Sam said, and I frowned past the pain in my face. It didn't feel like I was going to have a black eye, but it was sore. Kind of like when someone slaps you really hard.

"Why are you defending him? He's a scumbag."

"I'm not," Sam protested. "I'm just saying, I was his target, not you."

"That still doesn't make it okay."

"He's a bully," Conor said. "I doubt he cares whether it's boys or girls he hurts. Something needs to be done about him."

"When is anything ever done about bullies at this school? Teachers hear me being called a dyke every day of the week and they do nothing. And I'm not even gay, not that it matters," Amy put in, tucking her camcorder into her bag. I wondered if she'd caught any of the fight on tape, but then remembered she'd been talking to Conor when it happened. That was probably a good thing. I didn't want Dylan getting suspended, even though he was only defending me.

"We should get out of here. Yvonne's working tonight, so we can go back to my place," I suggested, wanting to get away from the school before anything else happened.

"Good idea." Sam nodded his enthusiasm. He wanted to leave the dance as much as I did. "We could try get some booze in the offo on the way."

"No off-licence is going to serve you," Amy scoffed. "You look about twelve."

She was right. Sam was five-four, blond, blue-eyed and skinny as a rake.

"It's a good job you three are eighteen then, isn't it?" Sam shot back with an arched brow.

"The booze is on me," Dylan said. "Come on. If I stay here any longer I'm in danger of going back in there." His tone was quietly firm, with an underlayer of anger, and I could tell he really hated Shane, maybe even more than the rest of us. Dylan struck me as the type to hate fiercely, but also to love just as fiercely. He felt all of life's emotions with everything he had in him, and there was a captivating sort of appeal about that.

The walk to the flats was mostly quiet, all of us stuck in our own thoughts. Dylan walked close beside me, his fingers touching mine every so often as though to check that I was all right. I wasn't, not really, but I could put up a good front. I'd never been punched before, and I was suffering from some aftershock.

It was like in the movies, when people got shot or bitten by a shark. It happened so quickly, there was a few moments where they didn't realise it had happened yet. The same went for being punched. It was so unexpected my brain was like, *Um . . . did I just get punched in the face?*

When we got to the off-licence, Dylan silently walked through the door, emerging a few minutes later with a bag. I kind of wanted to get drunk tonight. It'd help me forget how horribly wrong the dance had gone.

I slotted my key in the door and led everyone inside before I noticed Yvonne sitting on an armchair watching the telly, a glass of wine in hand. She had her hair up in a messy bun, make-up removed, and was wearing her comfy fleece pyjamas. My stomach dropped as a curious smile claimed her mouth.

"Well, hello everyone."

"Yvonne I, um . . ."

"You thought I'd be at work and came back to do some underage drinking in my flat. Yeah, I got that, Ev."

"I'm really sorry. It's just, the dance was horrible and—"

She waved away my explanation. "Oh, hush and come in. Introduce me to your friends."

Sam stepped forward and daintily offered his hand. "Samuel Kennedy the fifth, pleased to make your acquaintance."

Yvonne cast her eyes to the ceiling at Sam's antics and playfully shoved him aside. "I think we've already met, *Samuel*," she said. As she turned, a warm smile fell on Conor. "And I know Conor, too. He's our neighbour."

"Hi, Yvonne," he said, awkward and shy. I'd think it was adorable if I wasn't so embarrassed at being caught out.

"This is Dylan. He lives a few floors down. And Amy lives at the other end of the Villas," I said.

"It's nice to meet you both," said Yvonne, still smiling.

"So, how come you're not at work?" I asked. My aunt rarely missed a shift.

She gave a little sigh then gestured to her hand, which I now saw was wrapped in a bandage. "Right. I'm such a klutz. I dropped a glass at the bar, then cut myself when I tried to pick up the pieces. They sent me home for the night with a bandage and a few paracetamol, though they don't do much to help the pain."

"You should try codeine," Amy suggested. "Actually, Feminax works the best. You know, for period pain. When I want a nice, peaceful night's sleep I take two of those bad boys and I'm out cold."

"Oh, I might . . . try that. Thanks," said Yvonne, brow slightly arched.

"Are you going to be okay?" Conor asked, concerned.

"I'll be fine, hon. Nothing a glass of wine and some shuteye won't fix," she replied and took a sip.

"Do you mind if we drink these?" Dylan asked, gesturing to the bag of cans.

"You three, not at all. But these two," Yvonne replied, gesturing to Sam and me, "are underage, I'm afraid."

"Oh, Yvonne. Come on, let me and Ev have one drink. It's been a stressful night," Sam pleaded.

Yvonne frowned, her mothering instincts kicking in. "How has it been stressful? What happened?"

I flopped down onto the couch beside Sam and emitted a tired sigh. Dylan took the seat beside me, while Conor and Amy shared an armchair. "You know Shane Huntley? The boy who likes to give Sam a hard time at school?" Yvonne nodded. "Well, we were dancing and he came up and started picking on Sam, threatening him. I tried to intervene, and he swung around and punched me in the face."

"He what?" Yvonne exclaimed, a mix of anger and shock. She immediately rose from her seat and checked the damage. "I don't see any bruising, but we should ice it just in case. Sam, go grab the bag of frozen peas from the freezer." Sam hopped up right away, returning a moment later.

"He didn't realise it was me," I was quick to add, sucking in a harsh breath as Yvonne pressed the cold bag to my face.

"Yeah, and Dylan gave him a few jabs in Ev's defence," Sam added.

Yvonne's brows shot right up as she looked to Dylan. "You did?"

"I'd do it for anyone. No man should hit a woman," Dylan replied firmly.

"No, no man ever should," Yvonne agreed, looking from me and then to Dylan, coming to some sort of conclusion. She was dead wrong, of course. Dylan and I were just friends. Still, I knew what she was thinking when I saw the hint of a smirk on her face. "And what are your intentions towards my niece?"

I could've murdered her. "Yvonne!"

"What? He obviously has intentions. I'd just like to know what they are."

"We're friends. Leave it alone," I hissed.

"I think your niece is wonderful," Dylan blurted, and I could hardly contain my surprise. A blush claimed my cheeks.

Yvonne looked to me, clearly trying to hold back a grin. "And what you do think of him, Evelyn?"

"I think you need to shut your mouth," I responded, mortified.

"Well, that's no way to talk to your kind and lovely aunt, now is it?"

"It is when she's trying her best to embarrass me," I argued and turned to Dylan. "Don't mind her."

"Let's crack open these beers, shall we?" said Sam, doing me a solid. I shot him a look of thanks.

"You're not cracking open anything," Yvonne warned. "Not for another six months when it's your birthday."

Sam pouted. "Spoilsport."

"No underage drinking is allowed in this flat, and that's final."

Sam gave a huff and folded his arms, while I couldn't stop replaying Dylan's words in my head.

I think your niece is wonderful.

Never mind butterflies, there was a flock of sparrows in my chest, beating their persistent wings. I cast him a quick, speculative glance out the side of my eye and saw he was already studying my profile. I quickly looked away, bashful at being caught even though he was looking at me, too.

"So, you lot missed out on your dance. That's disappointing." Yvonne made a sad face. "I bet you were really looking forward to it and all."

Amy gave a mild scoff. "Eh, no. Dylan and I only went because Conor blackmailed us into it."

"I had to. You two are so anti-social. You never want to go to any of the dances."

"Oh, you like dancing?" Yvonne asked, turning to Conor.

I swore I could actually see the scarlet that coloured his caramel complexion. He glanced down shyly. "I know I don't look like the type, but yes."

"Not at all. You've got the look of a young Phil Lynott about you, and one of his most famous songs was 'Dancing in the Moonlight', so there you go."

"I'm not sure that makes sense, Vonny," Sam chuckled.

"'Course it does."

"No, he's right," Conor said, self-deprecating. "Nobody wants to see someone like me dancing."

"You can cut that sort of talk out right now," Yvonne chided. "Ev and I don't allow negativity in our flat, isn't that right?"

"Yep," I said, giving Conor a warm smile. "Plus, you've got that crazy cool afro." He seemed like he needed a pep talk. I wondered if he had his hopes set on becoming a social butterfly at the dance. Maybe kiss a girl for the first time. And then I had to go and ruin it by getting punched in the face by a homophobe.

71

"Girls don't like afros," he replied.

"Of course, they do. Ole Phil Lynott fought off the ladies, and you're the spitting image of him," Yvonne continued.

"That's because he was a rock star." Conor gave a soft sigh, though he seemed pleased by Yvonne's attention.

"And maybe *you'll* be a rock star one day. Do you play any instruments?"

Conor shook his head.

"Sing?"

He shook his head again. "I'm musically inept. All I'm good at is numbers. Dad wants me to become an accountant."

"Well, an accountant is a good job, and there's nothing women like more than a man with a good, stable income," Yvonne said.

"Do *you* like a man with a good, stable income, Vonny?" Sam asked cheekily, and Conor shot him a hard frown.

"'Course, I do," she replied. "Who doesn't?"

"Just wondering," Sam went on with a smirk.

"Well, anyway, I was just about to settle in and watch *When Harry Met Sally* if you lot want to join me."

"Oh, good Christ, not again," Sam groaned, while I reached out and gave his arm a light slap. "What?" he exclaimed. "She's seen it at least a dozen times."

"I've never seen it," said Dylan.

"Me neither," Conor added.

"Really?" Yvonne enthused. "Well then, you're in for a real treat."

"Yvonne is obsessed with this film," Sam told the others. "She's saving up to move to New York because of it."

"It's not all down to the movie," Yvonne corrected. "The city has always spoken to me. The iconography makes me feel like I could achieve anything I want there. That's why I'm going."

"When will you go?" Conor asked, brows drawn.

Yvonne blew out a slow breath. "On my salary? It'll take me another three years to save, I reckon. But at least Ev will be finished with school by then and making her own way in the world." She smiled warmly at me.

It was moments like these that I realised how lucky I was. There wasn't much less validating in life than your mam leaving you without a backwards glance. Yet somehow, Yvonne slipped into the role of carer, and I believed I thrived because of it. Sometimes I wondered how she could love me so much when I wasn't her own daughter. But she just did. I was lucky. She was aunt, confidant, friend, and my strongest cheerleader. As much as I wanted her to achieve her dream to move to New York, I wasn't looking forward to being separated.

Conor also appeared saddened by this news, but Yvonne didn't seem to notice. Instead she hit play on the DVD and the opening credits rolled.

"Billy Crystal, now there's a man with a questionable hairdo, and old Meggie Ryan is still interested," said Sam to Conor.

Conor shrugged, obviously still not convinced.

"Hush, or they'll miss the opening scene," Yvonne scolded, and he shut his mouth.

About thirty minutes into the film, while Meg Ryan was being particularly adorable with her shaggy nineties curls, and everyone was absorbed in the story, I got up to change into some PJs. I didn't notice Dylan followed me until I turned around and there he was in the doorway.

"Mind if I come in?" he asked, voice quiet.

I lifted a shoulder. "I've seen your room. I guess it's only fair that you see mine."

Dylan grimaced. "Sorry again, by the way, for being a prick."

"It's water under the bridge."

He stepped inside and sat on my bed, looking around with interest. I went to pull my pyjamas from the dresser. All I could think about was the fact that there was a boy sitting on my bed. A handsome, interesting, and slightly mysterious boy. His gaze traced the few trinkets on my shelf, lingering on the small vase of jasmine on my bedside table.

"Have you decided if you're going to go yet?"

I frowned at him. "Go where?"

"To New York, with Yvonne."

I let out a small sigh. "I can't. Not with my grandma living at the care home. If I went she'd have no one, and Yvonne deserves to finally pursue her dreams. She's spent the last four years of her life taking care of a teenager who isn't even hers."

Dylan studied me, his expression pensive. "So, you're just going to stay here at the Villas forever?"

I gave a soft chuckle. "You make it sound like a death sentence."

He was dead serious when he replied, "But it is."

"Oh, come on, this place might not be the Ritz, but it's hardly so bad. I've got a roof over my head, a garden to care for. Life doesn't always have to include some big, glamorous dream like it does for Yvonne."

"I think you're wrong."

I looked at him, fresh PJs hanging over my arm and said, "Okay, tell me how I'm wrong."

He chewed his lip, a deep frown marring his features. "Someone like you shouldn't stay in a place like this. If you do, you'll harden. Your attitude will sour. I hate it here. Every day I think about leaving. The only reason I stay is for Dad and to finish school."

The passionate way he spoke surprised me. I didn't think Dylan loved living here, no one did, but I hadn't realised he hated it so much either.

"Someone like me?" I whispered.

His reply was emphatic. "You're sunshine, Evelyn, and there's nothing but clouds around here."

I didn't know what to say, then Dylan continued, "I mean, do you ever think there'll come a day when you don't smell like this place? It seeps into all your clothes, all your stuff. Sometimes, when I meet new people, I worry they'll know where I come from just because of how I smell. Did you know I work weekends at a fragrance counter in Arnotts? It's where people with money go to shop, and some days I'm terrified they're going to figure it out. They're going to smell this place on me and know exactly where I come from. That I'm not one of them and I never will be."

I didn't know about Dylan's job, but he definitely had the looks to sell cologne to rich people. I still wasn't quite sure how to respond. I mean, what do you say to a speech like that?

"I just want to feel clean for one day in my life. I can never feel clean here."

"You are clean, Dylan. You're just overthinking it. You know, like how you say your dad does sometimes?"

"We both know I'm not. You and Yvonne might only allow positivity in your lives, but there's gonna come a time when you figure out it's all bullshit. The world is not a positive place, at least not when St. Mary's fucking Villas is your home."

My throat tightened, because now he was being mean. "That's not true," I whispered.

"What about your gran then? That's what we all have to look forward to. Getting old and having to face the indignity of not being able to go to the bathroom on our own."

"My gran is only fifty-nine," I told him, angrily. "She has MS. It's a degenerative illness. That's why she lives in a care home. Yvonne wanted to care for her here, but it just wasn't possible as her condition worsened. The lift is always out of order and we're six stories up. So please, get your facts straight before you talk about other people's situations."

Dylan stared at me, shamefaced, then looked down and wearily ran his hands down his face. "Fuck. I'm sorry. When I get started on these rants I just can't seem to stop sometimes."

I took a moment to calm down. Dylan hadn't intended to hurt me. In fact, it was clear he'd needed to vent his frustration. "You have a lot of anger in you."

His eyes rose to mine and he looked so tired, "I know."

"You're too young to be so angry."

He shook his head. "Anger can get you at any age, Ev, believe me."

I studied him a moment and wondered if it was because he lost his mam, if that was where his unhappiness stemmed from. Or maybe it was a product of growing up here, where a hundred small injustices built to a giant ball of dissatisfaction.

"So, what will you do after school?"

He lifted a shoulder. "Not sure yet."

"Really? You talk like you have some grand plan."

That got the tiniest hint of a smile out of him. "My grand plan is to get out of here. I'll figure out the rest when the time comes."

"Well, I think you've got worrying down pat. Perhaps you could become a professional misery merchant to people who have too much happiness in their lives. That is, when you're not hocking overpriced cologne and perfume to men and women who think they can spruce up their lives with a new scent."

He appeared interested by this last bit. "You think that's so absurd?"

"Not absurd. I just don't believe the latest fragrance from Calvin Klein is going to turn men into George Clooney, or women into Eva Longoria for that matter."

He huffed a breath of frustration. "Another thing we disagree on then."

I eyed him, incredulous. "You *do* believe that?" Dylan O'Dea was the last person I thought could be fooled by clever marketing ploys.

When he looked at me, his features transformed, like he was thinking of his absolute favourite place in the world. Or his favourite person. "I think scent can transform anything," he said, eyes aglow. "Take the Villas for example. If they didn't smell so bad, they wouldn't feel half as depressing. If they smelled like a field of wild lavender, or a grove of orange trees, I actually might not mind living here. If you ended up smelling sweaty and dirty after a shower, nobody would wash. Smelling nice makes people feel nice. It makes them feel ready to take on the day. I'll grant you, no, a fragrance can't turn a man into George Clooney, but it can make him *feel* like George Clooney, and that's why he's willing to pay so much for it."

As I listened to him speak, my heart started to beat faster. The way he spoke made me feel a sense of urgency, like I was watching a person race somewhere far beyond the horizon. I could try to follow, but I'd never be fast enough. Maybe that was the allure of Dylan O'Dea. He wasn't meant for a place like this, and he wouldn't be here long. I could feel it in my bones.

"I think I see how you got the job at Arnotts now," I said, my irritation fading as intrigue took its place.

This boy revealed something new and interesting every time we spoke, even if his negativity frustrated me.

"If there's one thing I'm good at, it's convincing people that smells are important."

"Makes sense, what with your nasal superpowers and all," I said, smiling.

We stared at one another for a moment. Dylan's gaze traced the waves of my hair that fell over my shoulders, the tight lines of my dress where it hugged my hips then flared out over my thighs. An unknown feeling swept over me, like I was burning up from the inside.

A buzz filled my tiny room and Dylan reached down to pull his phone out. He glanced at the screen then lifted it to answer.

"Dad, hey."

I watched as his brows formed a straight, furious line. "Right. I'll be there in a minute."

When he hung up he looked me dead in the eye, and I felt a chill at his expression. "Someone just spray-painted my fucking front door," he said, voice near a growl.

Without another word, he stalked out of my room and through the living room, where the others were still watching the movie.

"Hey, where are you going?" Amy asked, perplexed.

Dylan didn't answer but kept going until the front door slammed shut behind him.

"Someone spray-painted outside his flat," I explained, before hurrying after him.

Amy swore while Conor got up to follow me. Two minutes later all five of us were at Dylan's. A coil twisted in my gut when I saw the red letters on his door spelling out two words: *dead man*. Sam let out a gasp while I was the first to walk inside.

The scene I found struck a pang in my chest. Dylan knelt in front of the armchair where his dad sat, his arms tight around his neck as he hugged him. Tommy was obviously very shaken as Dylan whispered reassurances to try and calm him down.

"Whatever little shits did this deserve locking up," said Yvonne when she saw the state Tommy was in. She still wore her pyjamas, but she didn't appear to care right then. She walked over to Dylan and his dad, kneeling, too.

"Tommy, I'm Yvonne Flynn, Evelyn's aunt. Would you like me to call the Gardaí?"

Dylan's dad shook his head. "No, please don't. I don't want any trouble."

"They can't help anyway," said Dylan. "I'll sort this. You should all go home."

"We're not going home. And you're not sorting this on your own," Amy argued.

Something about her tone must've set him off, because he turned to her, furious. "If I say I'll sort it, I'll fucking sort it." A pause before his voice grew louder, sterner. "Now you all need to leave."

"But Dylan, we just want to—"

"I said LEAVE," he shouted, and I jumped in fright.

"Come on. Dylan's right," Yvonne said, the voice of reason. "We should give him and his dad some privacy."

I didn't want to go, but I also didn't want to contend with Dylan's rage. I think everyone was feeling the same way, because a moment later we were out, heading back to our flat.

"Do you think it was Shane?" I asked Conor as we walked. I could tell he was just as worried about Dylan as I was.

"I have no idea. It could've been some of the lads from the McCarthy gang. You know they've been trying to recruit him?"

I nodded. "Yeah, I saw the black eye he got for resisting."

Conor blew out a long breath. "They want him because of his size. They prefer lads like Dylan in their crew because he looks intimating to other gangs. Sometimes I'm glad to be skinny and half blind."

"You'll fill out," Sam said. "And there's always laser eye surgery. Also, I'm pretty sure this wasn't Shane. He's all talk and no teeth."

"He had some teeth when he was punching my niece in the face," Yvonne put in. "I'll be having a word with his mother the next time I see her."

"His ma's on crack," said Amy. "She could give a shit about what her son does."

Yvonne's mouth firmed, a small line forming between her eyebrows. "She'll give a shit when I'm finished with her."

"Go, Yvonne," Sam hooted. "You're our hero. I should get you a Wonder Woman costume for Halloween."

Conor's expression turned shy, like he was embarrassed for enjoying the idea of my aunt in costume. I think I was the only one who noticed though.

When we reached the flat, Yvonne pressed play on the movie, but I couldn't get into it. My mind was elsewhere. I couldn't stop thinking about Dylan and those horrible words on his door. His anger suddenly made sense. I couldn't imagine what it must be like having scumbags constantly taunting you, trying to wear you down. Only Dylan didn't strike me as the type to be worn down, and he seemed determined to drill the message home, whatever that entailed. My stomach felt tight and queasy as I imagined him digging an even bigger hole for himself.

What was he going to do? And more importantly, who exactly was he going to do it to?

Six

"You cleaned it off, didn't you?" came a voice over my shoulder.

I was on my way to class when Dylan gently grabbed my elbow, stopping me in place.

"Cleaned what off?" I asked, feigning ignorance as I looked up at him. Of course, I knew exactly what he was asking. Early this morning, I went to his flat and scrubbed the spray paint from his front door. I felt so useless, so unable to help, but I wanted to do *something*. So, I cleaned his door. It wasn't a big deal.

"Don't play coy. I know it was you. My dad saw you."

I blew out a breath. "Fine, it was me, but I wanted to do it. If it was Shane, then it's sort of my fault when you think about it."

"It wasn't Shane. He doesn't have the balls."

I thought on that a second. Maybe he was right. "Sam says he's all talk and no teeth."

"Sam talks a lot of sense . . . when the mood takes him."

I gave a soft laugh. "You're right about that."

Dylan smiled at me then looked away as we continued walking. He cleared his throat, a touch of emotion in his voice when he said, "Anyway, thank you for doing it. I would've cleaned it myself only I got so angry every time I looked at it. It was difficult not to punch a hole in the door."

"You probably could. Doors at the Villas are paper thin." I paused a second before I continued, "So . . . if it wasn't Shane, then who?"

Dylan's expression sobered. "You know who, Evelyn."

I lowered my voice and glanced around. "You're not going to join them, are you?"

"They'll have to kill me first," he replied darkly and a rush of anxiety went through me. It wasn't like the McCarthys hadn't killed people. And that was before you factored in all the drug-related deaths from the heroin they peddled.

"Don't say that," I whispered, stopping in place.

Dylan came to stand in front of me. He looked down and studied my expression. "Would you miss me if they did?"

"'Course I would."

My answer caused him some kind of pleasure, because his gaze heated and his features softened. "I better make sure I don't die then."

"Yes," I replied, rolling my eyes because he'd obviously been fishing for a compliment, or some clue as to my feelings. "Please do. Now I've got to get to class."

"Get to class then. And I'll be sure to keep this body of mine alive for ya," he said and reached out to squeeze my hand.

I stepped by him and continued down the corridor, my stomach fizzling from his brief touch. I was preoccupied during class, Dylan's smile in my head, his subtle flirting a thrill in my belly.

The next time I saw him was later that day in the lunchroom. I sat next to Sam and peeled back the cling film on my sandwich, when an almighty ruckus broke out.

All I could hear was, "FIGHT, FIGHT, FIGHT!" where a crowd had gathered at the other side of the room, but I couldn't see past all the students.

Sam's eyes grew big as he shoved back his chair and went to see who was fighting. I followed, mostly to make sure my friend didn't get caught in the crossfire. I pushed through bodies, all of them chanting, egging on whoever it was.

I froze when I saw Dylan fighting three other boys, all of them young McCarthy members. One of them, Jackson Keegan, was a known troublemaker. He was always getting suspended for fighting with other students, or trying to intimidate teachers. The sight of Dylan taking him on made my blood run cold, because it was rumoured Jackson had beaten one kid so badly he had to be hospitalised. Dylan was lucky he had brawn on his side.

When I left him earlier, he'd been so light-hearted and flirtatious. It was a shock to see him now, fighting off three boys with only his fists. He threw a punch at one, while another came from behind and kicked him in the shin. I winced and sucked in a breath. Dylan turned, and the boy who'd kicked him struck him again, this time in the chest.

"Hey! Break it up," the principal's voice boomed, and the crowd instantly dispersed. Mr Kelly was a formidable man. Over six feet tall with hair clipped short and a perennially stern expression, he wasn't the sort to be trifled with.

I walked a few yards away and watched as he pointed out Dylan and the others. "You four. My office. NOW."

A hush fell over the room while they were escorted out. I went to join Sam at our table, though I wasn't very hungry anymore.

"You think this is what Dylan meant when he said he'd sort it?" Sam asked, his mouth dipping downward. It was a rare occasion when Sam frowned, so I knew the fight had affected him.

"I'm not sure. They might've started it. He was probably trying to defend himself," I replied, anxious.

"I dunno. That boy seems to have a self-destruct button."

I exhaled heavily, because Sam was right. Dylan didn't strike me as someone who took self-preservation into consideration, especially when he felt threatened. He dove straight into the fray.

I was lost in thought when Shane walked by our table, his usual sneer in place.

"Can we help you?" Sam asked, a challenge.

"Nope. Just seeing what a pair of fags looks like."

"Girls aren't fags, fuckface. They're lesbos. Get it right," Sam retorted.

"A pair of lesbos then. Sometimes I forget what a little bitch you are."

Sam stood from the table, riled. "I'd rather be a little bitch than the son of a dirty crackwhore."

Shane blinked, and something like pain crossed his expression. A second later it was gone, his voice low and threatening when he spoke. "What did you just say?"

"You heard me."

At this, one of the teachers on supervision approached. "Is everything okay here?"

I swear, this school needed security guards. There was always a fight brewing somewhere. Shane and Sam eyed each other intently for a long moment, like two dogs about to go at it, then Shane cut the teacher a look.

"Everything's fine," he snapped and walked off.

The teacher retreated, probably glad to have quelled a second fight, and I glanced at Sam.

"You're starting to try your luck with him."

Sam ate a bite of his sandwich and mumbled, "Just getting sick of being pushed around."

I studied his expression and sensed there was something he wasn't telling me. It was troubling, because Sam had always been an open book. We didn't keep secrets from one another.

By the end of the day, word got around that all four boys involved in the fight had been suspended. I tried to find Dylan to check if he was okay, but he must've been sent home early.

I walked through the gates, planning on paying a visit to Gran on my way home, when he appeared from behind a fence. My hand went to my heart in fright.

"You scared me."

He scratched the side of his head, looking sheepish. "Sorry. I was waiting for you, but I didn't want to get spotted by any teachers. I've been suspended."

"Yeah, I heard. It's so ridiculous. It's not like you're the one who started the fight. You were only defending yourself."

He glanced away as his expression grew even more sheepish.

"Dylan," I gasped. "Please tell me you did not start a fight with three known gang members."

"They needed to see I mean business."

"Well, they mean bigger business. There's only one of you and who knows how many of them. It's not a fight you can win."

"I'm not giving up. I'd rather be dead than work for them."

"Oh, my goodness, can you please stop with all the death talk?"

"I told you, honesty is a problem for me."

"Yes, well, a little censorship every now and then wouldn't hurt," I sniffed.

It was confusing how much the idea of something happening to Dylan scared me. He wasn't anything to me. Well, he was a friend, just barely. I shouldn't be so terrified of him not being around anymore. I mean, he would probably leave at the end of the school year anyway.

"Where are you headed?" he asked, noticing I wasn't walking the usual way home.

"To visit my gran. You can come if you want."

"Okay," he said, and I glanced at him in surprise. Most people would pass on that kind of offer. Care homes weren't exactly the most enticing places to visit. At least he didn't seem to have any visible bruises from the fight. I wasn't sure the nurses would be too keen on letting a bruised-up teenager into the building.

"These homes always smell like piss and disinfectant," Dylan said as we walked inside and I waved hello to Zara, the receptionist. She knew Yvonne and me now, so she didn't make us sign in to visit anymore.

"Yep," I replied. "You don't need any heightened senses to smell that, unfortunately."

"There's an awful indignity to it," Dylan went on sadly.

"Very little dignity in sickness," I said, before knocking on the door to Gran's room.

"Come . . . in," she called, her words slow. Over the years her speech had deteriorated. Every time I noticed her condition worsen, I cried a little. It was amazing how you could cry without tears when you didn't want the other person to know you were upset.

I opened the door and stepped in, Dylan behind me.

"Hi, Gran. I hope you don't mind that I brought a friend along today. This is Dylan."

"I . . . don't mind. Hello, Dylan."

"Hello, Mrs Flynn. It's a pleasure to meet you," he replied and stepped forward.

"Oh . . . look . . . at you. Your . . . mother . . ."

"What's that, Gran?" I asked and pulled a chair up next to her wheelchair. She sometimes got a little

89

muddled when she tried to say things. Her thoughts were clear, but her body was incapable of articulating what she wanted to say. Some days she could speak perfectly fine, and then others she had trouble with basic sentences.

"You look just like your mother," Gran enunciated finally.

"You knew my mam?" Dylan asked, a catch of emotion in his voice.

Gran nodded ever so slightly. "We were neighbours at the Villas, and I used to work . . . as a florist. She bought flowers . . . from . . . me every week. Loved lilac."

Dylan closed his eyes for a second, his voice hushed when he replied, "Yeah, she did. She used to make me describe how they smelled all the time."

"How did you describe them?" I asked, eager to know.

"It's a strong, heady scent, sometimes cloying, but I love it because it reminds me of her so much. It can be very sweet, too."

"You really look . . . just like her," said Gran. "I'd recognise that face anywhere. It's uncanny. The lady . . . who couldn't smell who . . . loved flowers."

"Definitely ironic," said Dylan sadly.

"I'm sorry . . . to hear about her passing. She was taken too . . . soon."

Dylan nodded but didn't speak, his features solemn. I thought of my own mother and the new knowledge that it had been Dylan's parents who brought her to the hospital when she went into labour. I wanted to ask Gran about it, but wasn't sure how to bring it up.

In the end, I simply asked, "Have you heard from Mam lately?"

Gran nodded. "She . . . called . . . just last week. Said she's doing okay."

"Oh. That's good. Dylan's dad told me he was the one to drive her to the hospital when she had me. Do you remember?"

"Of course. It's the day you were born, after all. I was working . . . and Yvonne . . . was at school when it happened. There weren't mobile phones back then, so we didn't find out until she was hours into her labour."

I nodded thoughtfully, then asked, "What was she like, you know, back then?"

"My Lily? The opposite of you in every way. She was my wild daughter, and Yvonne was my little angel. But I loved them both the same." She paused to sniff. "Still do."

I knew it upset Gran how Mam left me, something she still struggled with. When I glanced at Dylan, he was studying me closely. I decided the conversation was getting too personal, especially with him sitting there, so I endeavoured to change the subject.

"Oh, by the way, Gran, did I tell you how well my bluebells are doing this year? I'm going to cut some to bring to you."

We chatted flowers for the next half hour, and I prepared tea and biscuits at the small kitchenette in Gran's room. Dylan watched me a lot, and he always seemed interested when I spoke about my allotment. I'd never known anyone to be so rapt by the subject. Even Yvonne was bored to tears by me at times.

It started to rain on our way home, so we had to run all the way back. I laughed when we finally got inside, because we were both soaked to the skin. Dylan leaned against a wall near the staircase, a faint smile on his lips.

"I don't want to go home yet," he said, and his expression sent a wave of pleasure through me.

"Why not?" I asked, my voice unexpectedly croaky.

"The school probably called my dad to tell him I was suspended, and I'm not ready to face him."

"Yvonne's at work. You can come up if you like. I'll make us something to eat."

His throat bobbed as he swallowed. "I'd like that."

I turned, and he followed me up the stairs. I somehow sensed him looking at my arse, but I didn't turn around to confirm it. A tingle skittered down my spine. When we reached the flat, I grabbed some towels from the airing cupboard to dry us off, then went to see what there was to cook for dinner. I popped a frozen pizza in the oven before joining Dylan on the sofa. He'd turned on the TV, and I noticed his knuckles looked a little red. The skin wasn't broken or anything, but it was probably painful.

Worrying my lip, I gestured to his hand. "That looks sore."

Dylan glanced down then flexed his fingers. "Yeah, hurts a little."

"Do you want some ice?"

"Nah, I'm good."

"A massage then?" I blurted.

He arched a brow. "A massage?"

I cleared my throat. "A hand massage, I mean. It probably won't do much to help the pain, but it's just something Sam and I do for each other when we're stressed. It's okay if you don't want one. I know some people don't like to be touched like that."

He gave a light chuckle. "Believe me, Ev. Any way you want to touch me, I'm certain I'll like it."

I had no reply for that, other than blushing furiously, so I just took his hand into mine. I liked how he called me Ev, the same as Sam and Yvonne did. His breath hitched a little as I started to knead his palm, and I momentarily regretted my offer. Touching him felt far more intimate than when I did this for Sam. With Sam it was friendly, but with Dylan there was something else. Something that made my chest ache and tingle at the same time.

"Feels good," Dylan said on an exhale. He sounded relaxed.

"I'm the best at hand massages," I said, then winced, realising my error. "I mean, uh, never mind."

His lips curved in a smile, but he didn't comment on my fluster. I continued to massage him, admiring how large his hand was, then imagining what he could do with it. The very thought heated my cheeks. I wondered if he'd had sex before. I mean, when you looked at him, it was easy to believe the opportunity had come along at some point. But was he experienced? How many girls had he been with?

Dylan let out an odd, groaning sound and I paused my movements to glance at him.

"I'm sorry. Did I hurt you?"

"You definitely aren't hurting me," he replied.

"Oh. Okay. Good."

Tentatively, I started to massage him again, but I felt more self-conscious than before. Me touching his hand was hardly turning him on, but the way he looked at me . . .

I glanced at him again and he was staring at my mouth. I turned away quickly, pulse thrumming, then asked a question that had been weighing on my mind.

"Dylan?"

"Hmm?"

"Why do you think I'm wonderful?"

His voice was slow, almost sleepy now. "Think you're—"

"You told Yvonne the other night that you think I'm wonderful. I was just wondering why." My words came out in a rush.

He was silent for a long moment, and I pushed my finger down the centre of his palm. He emitted a sound of pleasure, and there was something about touching him that made me feel peaceful and electric all at once.

Finally, he answered, "When you smile at people and say hello, you really mean it."

Was that it? Disappointment filled me. Somehow, I was expecting something a little less . . . mundane.

"I think most people mean it when they say hello, Dylan."

"Not like you do. You have this glow, this inner spirit that makes me feel . . . I don't know, lighter somehow. Like, it reassures me there's still good in the world," he explained, and a fluttery sensation claimed my chest. Maybe his reason wasn't so mundane after all. His expression turned a little shy as he continued, "How you look doesn't hurt either."

My voice became a whisper as curiosity overtook me. "How do I look?"

He hesitated, considered his answer, then spoke with a fervency I'd never seen in him. "You look like a sunny day at the beach when you get sand in your toes and build sandcastles. And when your dad is happy instead of freaking out over every creak he hears from the floorboards, thinking it's woodworm, rats, or a serial killer hiding in the closet."

"Oh, um, thanks, I guess," I said, frowning. I knew what he said was a compliment, but it was such an odd way to put it. I worried for him. Worried he was too young and too full of potential to always be so weighed down.

He swore under his breath, shaking his head. "Wait, that came out wrong. What I mean to say is, you look like a life away from here. A happy life. And you're the most beautiful person I know, so there's that."

I stared at my lap for a second, heart racing. No one had ever said anything like that to me. Not even close. "I have no idea where you get these high opinions of me," I said shyly.

"Maybe it's because I've always watched you. I can't remember a time when I didn't."

"I've only lived here a few years," I said, backtracking through my memories, to all the times when I'd noticed Dylan around. I studied them through a microscope, trying to rewind and hit playback in slow motion.

I remembered one day when I'd first started living with Yvonne. I was carrying groceries home and put the bags down for a second to rest my hands. When I glanced to the side, there was a boy hanging out by the staircase. *Dylan*. He'd looked at me like he'd wanted to say something, maybe offer help with the bags, but instead shook his head, turned around and walked away.

He was telling the truth. He had watched me, and had often looked me in the eye. Before now I didn't pay it much attention, just thought he was a staring sort. Now I was looking on it all in a new light.

"When you still lived with your mam and only came to the Villas to visit your aunt and gran, I watched you then, too. You always seemed so happy. I thought life with such a happy girl must be a pretty sweet life to live."

It was true. I'd always been cheerful. Not to the point of irritating people, but I liked to think I was a positive person. The exact opposite of Dylan, you might say. Maybe that was why we interested one another so much.

"That's a very nice thing to say," I finally replied, my thoughts flustered. His attention was making my skin feel too warm.

His lips quirked when he responded, "I'm a very nice person."

I narrowed my eyes at him playfully. "No, you're not."

His attention went to my lips again, this time with intent. "No, you're right, I'm not," he murmured, right before he took my face in his hands and kissed me. I gasped into his mouth, completely blindsided, hands fumbling for something to hold on to.

I'd never been kissed before, so my movements were awkward, sloppy. Dylan seemed to know what he was doing, because he tilted my head to get a better angle. And then . . . and then . . .

And then he slid his tongue into my mouth. It felt slippery and wet, but the way it moved was like a massage, a little like how I'd been tending to his hand a few moments ago. A tingling sensation travelled throughout my body as a tiny whimper escaped me. Something about the noise made Dylan kiss me harder, his tongue speeding up as he moved over me. He shifted closer until my back was flat to the couch, and he held himself above me.

I grasped at his shoulders, lips still unsure, and tried to match the way he kissed me. Tentatively, I slid my tongue against his, and he emitted a low, sexy groan. I trembled. I tried again, and again he groaned, this time palming my thighs and pulling them apart. He settled himself between my legs, and the stiffness in his pants panicked me.

I didn't break the kiss though. I was far too eager for it, and I didn't want the moment to end. Who knew if he'd ever kiss me again? I needed to make this last, so I could etch his taste into my memory, fold his smell in crepe paper and save it for a rainy day when I needed some sunshine.

That's what he tasted like—bottled sun. Golden, like the flecks in his hair.

Time passed, but he didn't break our kiss. Not even to catch his breath. It felt like he didn't want this to end either. Like he'd been waiting his entire life for this kiss, and nothing or nobody was going to rush him. His mouth warmed my mouth. The way his tongue moved made my entire body feel hot and languid, like I could melt into the sofa.

The kiss grew more and more frenzied, until he pushed his hard crotch firmer between my thighs, his hips moving in a way that built a pleasure in me. A coil of thick arousal coated my insides, and a sharp, luxurious sensation filled my entire lower half.

Dylan licked and nipped at my lips, making low, masculine sounds to match my keening whimpers. I didn't know what I was doing, but I knew I liked it. Kissing him made me feel whole, even though I'd never known there was a piece missing.

I wanted to feel his erection with my hand, undress him and explore the possibilities of his body. I wanted to know what he looked like naked.

I squeezed my thighs around his hips, pushing into him, needing something I couldn't quite describe. My skin was hot and flushed, my breath fast like I'd run a marathon, and my heart felt like it was beating a million times a second.

Between my legs an acute pleasure built. To what, I didn't know. But I did know that if *it* didn't happen soon I might spontaneously explode.

Dylan's erection rubbed against the seam of my pants, but I wished for it to rub harder. I wished for him to slip that large hand of his inside and feel my skin. He groaned again and something about the sound combined with the friction sent me over the edge. Starbursts, fireworks, and comets went off behind my eyes. I squeezed them shut and shook as several wonderful tremors took my body.

It was a few long moments before I opened my eyes and Dylan stared down at me, his gaze dark with lust.

"Did you just . . .?"

I shook my head and bit my lip. "Nope. Nu-uh. Definitely not."

But I did. I *so* fucking did.

I just had my very first orgasm.

That had to be it, because if it wasn't, then an actual orgasm must be something truly mind-blowing indeed.

I couldn't believe he made me come without taking any of my clothes off. Without touching me. He'd only been kissing me.

"Jesus," Dylan rasped then dropped his head into the crook of my neck. After a moment, he began planting kisses along my skin, and I heated right up again. Again, his lips found mine, and just like before, I didn't want to stop. Not to take a breath. Not for nothing.

We kissed until our lips were sore.

We kissed so long I'd taste him on my tongue for days.

Then I heard a key slot in the door, and it all ended. Dylan and I snapped apart like we'd just been electrocuted. He sat up straight on the other end of the couch, while I went to the kitchen to check on the pizza. It was a little burned, but still edible.

"Oh Ev, you will not believe the day I had," Yvonne said as she walked in then paused. "Oh . . . hello, Dylan."

He scratched his head, a touch embarrassed. "Hi, Yvonne."

"I invited Dylan over for something to eat. I hope that's okay," I said, feeling flushed. My eyes found Dylan's for a moment and butterflies flooded my belly before I looked to my aunt. She studied me, like she saw something different, and I worried she could see the entire past thirty minutes with that one look: the orgasm Dylan had given me and the way he made my skin feel too tight for my body.

Her eyebrow slowly rose, as it was prone to do. "That's fine. Have you eaten yet?"

Relief flooded me as Yvonne went to hang up her coat and bag. "Not yet. There's pizza in the oven. Want some?"

She sighed. "I'd love some. And I can tell you both all about the crazy old man who came to the bar trying to buy whiskey with Irish pounds. I actually think this was the first time he left the house in four years and no one told him about the euro changeover."

"He must've left the house," Dylan said. "How else would he buy food?"

Yvonne paused to consider the question. "Maybe he lives on a farm and grows his own."

"He'd still need supplies. Four years is a long time," Dylan countered, and Yvonne took a seat, smiling as she settled in for a debate. My aunt loved peculiar conversations. I was happy to let the two of them battle it out, because I needed some time to think about THE KISS. I was trying my best to seem relaxed, while on the inside I was entirely discombobulated.

God. How the boy kissed. I felt like I was floating. I'd never had girlfriends I could talk to about boys, hadn't felt I needed any. But I was completely thrown. *Dylan O'Dea freaking kissed me.* He more than kissed me. He devoured me as if there hadn't been a choice. Had he wanted to touch my body like I'd wanted to touch his? Was his mind going round and round in circles wondering what it could have led to?

Then, when I glanced at him, his eyes met mine for a second, and a pleasurable chill ran through me.

Yeah, he was definitely thinking about it, too.

Seven

"Do you think everybody's redeemable in some way?" Sam asked as I tended to my flowers. He must've been bored because he'd decided to come up and join me. It was a Sunday, late evening, and I hadn't seen Dylan all week. Not since our couch fumble.

I wondered if his dad grounded him for getting suspended; he didn't seem the type. Maybe he regretted kissing me and was keeping his distance until he figured out a way to let me down easily.

Such was the way my mind worked when it began fretting about things.

"Redeemable?" I asked, only half paying attention.

Sam let out an impatient sigh. "You've been in your own little world all week. What's up with you?"

I'd been hesitant to tell him about Dylan, mostly out of pettiness. I could tell Sam had some sort of secret, something he wasn't telling me. I wasn't going to confide in him if he wouldn't confide in me.

"If I'm in my own little world, you're in your own little universe," I replied.

Sam tilted his head. "What's that supposed to mean?"

"You've been just as distracted as I have, and what's all this about people being redeemable? Who exactly are you talking about?"

Sam looked away, something akin to shame on his face. He took a long moment to consider his answer, then finally he blurted, "Shane kissed me."

I blinked at him. "He what?"

He turned away again, his expression conflicted. "He kissed me. You were right. He is gay."

More blinking. I was stunned, couldn't believe what I was hearing. Couldn't believe both Sam and I had our first kisses within the same week. And now I understood his question. He wanted to know if *Shane* could be redeemed.

I considered how to phrase my question. "So . . . um, how did it happen?"

"He cornered me on the way home from school one day. You were gone to visit your gran, so I was on my own. I was so scared, thinking he was going to hit me or something, but then he just . . . grabbed me and kissed me."

My mouth fell open. My Freudian theory turned out to be true, and I hadn't really believed in it myself.

"Wow."

"Yeah," Sam sighed. "So now I have to deal with the fact that my bully has a crush on me."

"Quite the pickle," I said, chewing on my bottom lip. A silence fell between us before I ventured, "How was it?"

Sam squinted at me. "The kiss? Horrible. Completely and positively gross."

I chuckled. "That good, huh?"

He sighed again. If he wasn't careful people might mistake him for a dejected eighteenth-century damsel waiting for a husband. "What is it about bastards we can't resist?"

I shrugged, no answers forthcoming. I'd never fancied a bastard. Quite the opposite. I fancied Dylan O'Dea, who talked about things most people our age never gave a second thought, and told me I was beautiful inside and out.

Almost as though my thoughts conjured him, he appeared on the roof with Conor by his side.

"Looks like we have company." Sam knocked back a gulp of his Coke.

I caught Dylan's eye. His smile was so radiant, all my worries from the last week evaporated. He hadn't stayed away by choice. Indifference wasn't something boys felt when they smiled at girls like Dylan O'Dea was smiling at me.

I hoped.

"Thought we'd find you up here," he said, coming to sit on the edge of my allotment. Conor sat, too, saying hello to Sam.

"No Amy today?" Sam asked, and Dylan shook his head.

"She's visiting her cousins in Wexford."

"A pity. I'm becoming fond of her snark."

"She tells it to you straight, that's for sure," Conor agreed.

"So, what are you two handsome fellas up to this evening?" Sam asked, fluttering his eyelashes flirtatiously.

"Thought we'd gatecrash whatever you two are doing," Dylan replied, looking at me. "This is the first I've been out since I got suspended."

So, his dad *was* the grounding type. I swallowed my relief, while memories I'd been replaying all week flooded my head.

"Freedom looks good on you," I muttered under my breath and Dylan's eyes crinkled in another smile.

"Well, once Ev's finished up here we're gonna work on a sugar high, then binge-watch *Desperate Housewives*," said Sam.

"But you're both very welcome to join us," I added quickly.

Sam cut me a look, questioning why I was being overly friendly. I mean, I was. But I wanted Dylan to stay. I feared Yvonne walking in on us the other day scared him off. My aunt knew something was up, perceptive as she was, and proceeded to interrogate Dylan over burnt pizza and 7up.

Funnily enough, she didn't say much to me after he left, only that she knew I was a clever girl and didn't need to be warned about being 'careful'. Somehow it came out sounding like a warning anyway.

"Need any help?" Dylan asked and scooted closer to me, his voice soft.

"Nah, I'm almost done here," I replied, just as softly.

What I really wanted to say was, *you can help me by kissing me again.*

Seriously, laying a kiss as amazing as that on a girl and then leaving her hanging for a full week was just plain rude.

"Hey, maybe one of you can help me with a question," Sam said to Dylan and Conor.

"I love questions," Conor commented dryly.

"Well," Sam went on, unfazed, "I was wondering whether you think everyone is redeemable?"

"Everyone in the whole entire world?" Dylan asked incredulous. "Definitely not."

"Okay." Sam gave him his full attention. "Why?"

"You have serial killers, paedophiles, rapists, all of whom continually reoffend, even when people try to help them rehabilitate."

"All right, I'll give you the serial killer and the rapists, but what about people who are just sort of arseholes? Do you think they can ever become less . . . arsehole-y?"

I chuckled at Dylan's perplexed expression. He was quiet a moment, thinking on it, then said, "I suppose under the right conditions, if they actually wanted to change, then yes, they could be redeemed."

"Huh," Sam said, mulling it over.

"A lot of people have their reasons for being who they are. Some are just too far gone," Dylan went on. "Take my dad as an example. He's always been a worrier, probably since the day he was born. It's just how he is. He'll never change, no matter if all the evils in the world were suddenly eradicated. He'd still worry that the sun might shine too brightly, or that the moon could fall from the sky."

"Some people take pleasure in fretting," I added.

"Exactly," Dylan agreed. "In my opinion, we've all got an inherent negativity bias, something inside of us that makes us fixate on the bad rather than appreciate the good. It's certainly a problem for me."

"Isn't that just an Irish thing though? A weird by-product of a conquered people?" Conor suggested. "We're programmed to fixate on dark clouds. And my dad is Kenyan, so I'm double screwed," he joked.

Dylan considered him a moment, thinking on it. "Remember in *The Matrix*, when Agent Smith tells Morpheus the first matrix was a utopia, and it fell apart because the humans couldn't accept it? We define our existence through misery and suffering. He said the perfect world was a dream we kept trying to wake up from, too good to be real. I think that's all of us, no matter what country we're born into."

I frowned at him now. "I'm sorry, but I don't agree. I don't define my existence through misery, I define it through the people I love."

Dylan's attention landed on me, his expression contemplative, and I thought he wanted to say something but then Sam asked, "What's a negativity bias?"

Dylan glanced at him, and if I wasn't mistaken he appeared somewhat relieved for the distraction. He pushed up his shirtsleeve to the elbow, revealing an attractive forearm. It was an unconscious action, but it transfixed me. I found everything about his body interesting, from the tiny freckle above his upper lip, to the small stress line between his eyebrows. I felt like some Victorian-era gentlemen, who got a stiffy from the sight of a bare ankle.

"Okay, so imagine something bad happened, and then right after it, something good. You'd still be upset by the bad thing, even though the good thing came right after," Dylan explained.

Sam's expression was thoughtful, and he went quiet. Finally he said, "This one time, Mrs Gogarty gave me a right rollicking when I failed the French exam, and I couldn't stop thinking about how mean she was even though it was my birthday the next day and everyone was giving me presents."

"What an adorable example, Sam," I said on a chuckle.

He shot me the side-eye and stuck out his tongue.

"For most people it's fine, they can get over their pessimistic thoughts eventually. But some of us, well, we can get trapped for days in negative thinking. It can be quite damaging to your mental health," Dylan continued.

"Do you know what? We always talk about the most unusual things when you're around," Sam told him.

Dylan gave a wry smile. "I'll try to take that as a compliment."

Sam was right though. Dylan had this way of making you think about things that might never normally cross your mind. I knew he thought he depressed people, but I found him captivating. I liked getting his take on things, which was why I wanted to ask him what he thought about Shane kissing Sam. I was worried Sam might get carried away with whole forbidden nature of it all. Shane was good-looking, but he was still a bully, and he was a very, very angry and troubled individual. Combine that with a bad case of self-deception and an inability to accept his sexuality, you had a recipe for disaster, with Sam in the eye of the storm.

I nudged my friend with my elbow. "Can I tell Dylan and Conor about what you just told me?"

Sam gaped at me. "What? No!"

"Okay, now I'm curious," Conor said. "What did he tell you?"

"I want to get their opinions. And they won't tell anyone, right?" I looked from Dylan and then to Conor.

"Cross my heart," Conor assured.

"I need a little more information before I can make that promise," Dylan countered with a smirk.

"Oh, don't be difficult," I chided, unable to help smiling back at him.

He raised his hands. "Fine. I won't tell a soul. These lips will go to their grave sealed."

Great, now I was thinking about his lips.

Sam gave a beleaguered groan. "Okay, you can tell them, but you both seriously need to promise not to tell anyone, especially Amy. She won't be able to keep her mouth shut, and if this gets out I'm dead."

I thought he was being a tad overdramatic there, but whatever. I looked from Conor to Dylan. "Shane Huntley kissed him the other day."

"Piss off," Conor scoffed, disbelieving.

"Doesn't shock me," Dylan said.

"Well, it shocks me," Conor disagreed. "Shane's just so . . . not gay." A pause as a thought crossed his face. "He's the anti-gay."

I laughed softly at his fervency, while Sam eyed Dylan curiously. "Why doesn't it shock you?"

"Oh, come on," Dylan scoffed. "He's the very embodiment of a self-hating gay. A prime example of growing up in this place. Anger, violence, and overt masculinity are revered, while anything even remotely effeminate in a man is considered repugnant. It's pretty standard in lower socio-economic groups."

"Sometimes you talk like a professor studying the Villas instead of someone who actually lives here," Sam said, and he was dead right. It felt like Dylan had already mentally removed himself from this place. He'd made up his mind to leave a long time ago, and nothing would stop him from going. I felt a faint pang of missing him, and he wasn't even gone yet.

"It's easier to live here that way," he replied, and Sam studied him with narrowed eyes.

Like me, Sam was pretty accepting of his place in life. He didn't have any wild or lofty aspirations. He just wanted to a job, a roof over his head, and somebody to love him.

"My mam says this was the fifth-last place God made. It's bad, but it's not the worst," said Sam.

"That's a good way of putting it," Conor agreed.

"Anyway, I think you should be careful where Shane's concerned. He's not right in the head," Dylan warned.

"Who would be right in the head when they were raised by a mother like his, though?" Sam questioned.

Was he defending him?

110

"Well, like I said, some people are dicks because someone else made them that way," Dylan told him, *almost* apologetically. He seemed to see the hope in Sam and wanted to let him down gently. I tried to deal with the fact that Sam obviously wanted Shane to be redeemable. I mean, it made sense. This was the first bit of romantic attention he'd received from another boy, and I used the term 'romantic' very loosely. He wanted it to be real. I could only imagine the star-crossed lovers narrative going on in his head right now.

Down on the street, there was a loud ruckus as a bunch of people got off the bus coming into town. They were all young, all dressed to the nines for their Saturday night out. A pair of sparkly high heels caught my eye, twinkling in the fading daylight. Dylan let out a low grunt of displeasure when he saw them.

"What's wrong?" I asked, frowning at his sudden annoyance.

He shook his head. "Nothing. Never mind."

"No, you're obviously bothered about something. Tell us."

He blew out a breath. "They just irritate me."

"Who? The people who got off the bus?"

"Look, I know it's irrational," he huffed. "But I just can't stand people who come into the city to get drunk."

"They can be pretty irritating," Sam agreed. "Most weekends I get woken up at three in the morning by people making noise on their way home from the nightclub down the street. Pisses my dad right off, too."

Dylan's jaw moved in a way that told me he was agitated. "It's all fun and games for them to come in

111

here and mess around. Have fun. Be loud. Act like fools because they're anonymous in the city. They don't realise that some of us actually have to live here," he fumed, a deep frown marring his forehead. "We don't get to go home to our big suburban houses and sleep off the hangover. Our lives are a constant hangover. Our homes aren't houses, they're shelves. Worse than shelves, they're units, containers. They slot us in, making sure we take up as little space as possible. Making sure it costs them as little as possible, with cheap materials, and dodgy wiring, and pyrite, and mould and radon. We have no gardens to sit in, nothing pleasant to look at. Just concrete and dust and noise and dreams so big that one day we might crack in half from trying to hold them all in."

I had to catch my breath when he finally finished talking, because my heart was racing. I wasn't sure what it was about what he said, but I felt angry, too. I felt angry just from listening to him. It was like he gave voice to things I never even realised agitated me. But they did. I knew it by the way my chest burned.

We did live in containers.

Cheap, dirty, and grey.

And we didn't have gardens.

Hell, I had to go so far as creating my own on this dank, rust-infested roof to sate my need to be around nature. To see green things and colour. And there was the constant fight against mould and various other hazards of living in a badly constructed building.

"But this is what you get when you're at the bottom," Conor pointed out. "You have to work your way up. Nobody gets given anything for free in life."

"That's not true. The rich get everything for free, and they're the ones who need it least," Dylan countered. "With their tax cuts and expense accounts, and complimentary tickets to go see Bon Jovi play some ridiculously giant arena."

"Okay, you have a point," Conor acceded.

"And they don't appreciate any of it," Dylan grunted. "I tell you what, if I ever make any kind of money, I'll be grateful for every penny, and I won't keep it all to myself like a selfish bastard either."

"People always say that," Sam said. "But then they win the lotto, and poof, they think they're Mariah and could give a shit about the people who were there for them before the money came along. You see stories about it in magazines all the time."

"Well, I won't be like that. Just you wait."

I eyed him, feeling speculative. "How can you be so sure you'll make it rich? More people fail than succeed."

And more specifically, *how* did he plan on doing it? I swear I could sit for hours asking him questions, picking his captivatingly interesting brain.

Dylan shook his head. "I'm not sure. I'm just determined."

"And if you succeed, will you be happy then? Or will you be like your dad, worrying that the sun is shining too brightly, or that the moon might fall from the sky?" I asked in challenge.

113

Dylan seemed surprised that I was able to quote him so exactly. But when he spoke, I listened, soaked up every word. He studied me for a long time, and I couldn't tell if he was irritated by my question or if it gained me a new level of respect from him.

I decided it was the latter when his expression warmed as he replied, "Honestly? I don't know. But that doesn't mean I won't try."

A short silence fell, and I stared at Dylan. I couldn't tell how long I was locked in his gaze when Sam spoke. "Okay, let's talk about something a little cheerier, eh? Name three of your favourite things. Ev, you go first."

I grinned at Sam. I loved how he always found a way to brighten the mood. "Hmm, let me see," I said, pondering it as I scratched my chin. I lifted a finger. "Little old dogs with fat bellies who waddle when they walk up to you on the street." I lifted a second finger. "Babies laughing at their own farts." I lifted a third. "And the smell of jasmine first thing in the morning."

"Babies laugh at their own farts?" Conor asked, perplexed.

I nodded. "Yes, it's both hilarious and adorable."

"My little brother Mark used to do it all the time," said Sam. "Okay, Conor, it's your turn now. Go!"

Conor scoffed. "That's easy. My three favourite things are meat feast pizzas, the Discworld series by Terry Pratchett, and the way Yvonne looks when she smiles at me." He appeared a little embarrassed by the last bit.

I shook my head at him. "I can't believe you're still crushing on my aunt."

114

"After he saw her in her PJs last week his crush reached stratospheric levels," Dylan told us.

"You're one to talk," Sam commented. "I bet one of *your* favourite things is the way Ev looks when she smiles at you."

Dylan cast me a glance, and I flushed when he replied, "It might be."

"*Sigh*. He's so romantic. Isn't he romantic, Ev?"

"My God, Sam. You already sigh way too much, you don't need to introduce the actual word into your repertoire," I complained, trying not to blush.

"Oh hush, you love everything in my repertoire."

I rolled my eyes. He was right. I did. There was something in my DNA that programmed me to adore him, even when he was irritating the crap out of me. I was still thinking about my best friend when Dylan spoke, but instead of addressing all of us, he directed his words to me.

"My other two favourite things are how your eyes look like sapphires in the sunlight, and the way you laugh when someone says something really funny."

I looked at him then, and my heart caught in my throat. There was no inhibition in his eyes, no hesitation in talking to me so intimately with Conor and Sam beside us. My entire body grew hot as I looked away shyly, wishing we were alone, wishing I could kiss him.

"Anybody got a fan? 'Cause I'm swooning my arse off over here," Sam thrilled, fanning himself with his hand. "They should hire you out for hen parties. Who needs a stripper when they could have you serenading them with flowery love talk?"

Yes, who indeed.

Something unfurled inside me, a fleshy, curly, tangled thing. It twined itself around my heart, my lungs and other organs, twisting tight until I felt like I couldn't breathe too well.

And it sucked, because he'd never stay here. *With me*. Dylan was meant for more than this tiny city on the edge of a little island surrounded by the sea.

And just like a rock hurtling off that very edge, I fell for him hard.

Eight

I couldn't look at Dylan, not until I made sense of all these feelings.

Thankfully, Sam came to my rescue again when he suggested we go downstairs to make a start on those *Desperate Housewives* episodes. I quickly gathered my things, and we went to the flat. Dylan walked close beside me, his fingertips brushing mine when he bent to whisper in my ear, "Are you all right?"

I nodded fervently. "Absolutely fine."

"You're very quiet."

I flicked my gaze to his for a brief second. "Got a lot to think about."

We reached the flat, and I let everyone in. Yvonne would be at work until the early hours, so I wasn't worried about her walking in on us. I let Sam fire up the DVD player as I went into the bathroom to scrub the soil from my fingers.

"You've always got dirt under your nails."

Dylan gave me a fright when he spoke. He stood in the doorway, watching me.

"Yvonne says I'm constantly busy tending to some plant or other. Dirty fingernails are an occupational hazard." I tried to sound casual while his words echoed off the walls of my skull.

My other two favourite things are how your eyes look like sapphires in the sunlight, and the way you laugh when someone says something really funny.

Seriously, was he trying to steal my heart and run away with it? Sell it for the money to start a life away from the Villas?

"That wasn't a criticism. It suits you. You always smell like green things. Leaves and wet earth."

"Bet that's another of your favourite things," I muttered under my breath.

"What's that?"

I let out a frustrated groan as I dried off my hands. "Seriously, you need to stop being so nice to me."

He tilted his head. "Would you prefer me to be mean?"

"Yes," I exclaimed. "If you're so dead set on leaving after you finish school, then I would absolutely prefer you to be mean." A pause as my voice became a whisper. "It'll save me the broken heart."

I tried to walk by him then, but he grabbed my wrist. With his other hand, he tilted my chin up, forcing my gaze to his. He didn't breathe a word, just continued to study me with his microscopic eyes. A long, long few moments passed, and I was surprised Sam didn't come to check we hadn't fallen through the plughole.

When Dylan finally spoke, his words created a yearning ache in my gut. "There's a simple solution for that, you know."

I arched an eyebrow. "Oh?"

"Come with me."

For the tiniest second, my heart stopped beating. I shook my head and walked away from him, dismissing the idea. He followed me to the kitchen. Conor and Sam sat in the living room, watching us walk by.

"I can't do that. I have to stay for Gran."

"That's ridiculous. Your gran wouldn't want you to waste your life in this place. I know she wouldn't."

I barked a laugh. "You spent one evening with her and now you know her so well?"

"Yes, actually. It's easy to see the good in people, just as it can be easy to see the bad."

"Well, I don't consider a life here a waste like you do."

As soon as the words were out, I knew they were a lie. Dylan's speech from earlier was still burning through me. It sparked a fire, a dissatisfaction with the shitty lot we'd been handed. I hated it. I didn't want to feel dissatisfied. I wanted to feel happy, content . . . positive. That was the person I'd always been.

Dylan O'Dea was changing me in all sorts of ways, he was showing me new ways to think, and as futile as it might be, I fought against it tooth and nail.

"You're wrong. It is a waste," he said, voice firm. He so thoroughly believed in his own propaganda, it was maddening.

My lips formed a thin line. "Well, we'll just have to agree to disagree on that one."

With that, I grabbed the stash of junk food Sam and I had set aside and walked out into the living room. I dumped the bag of crisps and chocolates down on the coffee table, then grumpily told Sam to hit play.

He raised both eyebrows and uttered a quiet, "*Oookay* then," before he tapped the button on the remote.

To my annoyance, Dylan didn't give me a wide berth. Instead he came and sat right next to me, folded his arms, and stared at the TV screen. I knew he'd probably prefer to be watching a documentary on the Discovery Channel, instead of some trashy U.S. comedy-drama. A little of my irritation faded when he watched it anyway without complaint.

And that's what true friends did. But I had to pause at that thought, because before now, I hadn't thought of Dylan as my friend. *But he'd become one, and one so important to me.* We weren't even boyfriend and girlfriend, and he wanted me to leave with him. Did he really want that?

I didn't say a word for almost four episodes, and Sam kept casting curious glances my way. I wasn't the sort of person to have spats or be angry in general. It took an awful lot to piss me off, but the way Dylan thought I should just leave my gran so I could swan off and live an exciting life was infuriating.

I wasn't my mam.

I wouldn't be selfish like her and run away from my responsibilities.

I was going to let Yvonne have her chance. Good, kind, selfless Yvonne, who took me in when my mam would've handed me off to social services to live in some group home. She deserved to fulfil her dreams.

And I, well, I could be happy here. Once Dylan's opinions faded and became no more than a distant, forgotten memory, I was sure I'd be happy.

I'd focus on what I had and be content, rather than yearning for things in other places.

"Well, I think I'm ready to hit the hay," Sam said with a yawn. "No more housewife shenanigans for me tonight."

"Yeah, I better get home, too," Conor added. "School tomorrow, and all that."

I walked them to the door, giving Sam our customary hug goodbye and shooting Conor a brief parting smile. I expected Dylan to leave with them, but he hung back. He looked like he had a lot on his mind.

"Can we talk?"

"What's there to talk about?"

His gaze didn't waver. "Us."

I cocked a brow. "*Is* there an us?"

"There is for me," he replied gravely.

I blew out a breath and closed the door, then walked into the kitchen to put the kettle on. "I'll make tea then."

"I don't want tea."

I glanced at him, frustrated. "Goodness, Dylan, you don't have to drink it. It's only tea. You can sit and stare at the cup for all I care."

"Okay," he said and pulled out a chair.

I turned around, fiddling with mugs and spoons and hoping he'd talk so I wouldn't have to. He didn't, so I let out a weary sigh as I turned to face him, grasping the edge of the countertop.

"I was happy with my life before you came along."

His expression was stoic. "People who think they're happy aren't thinking hard enough."

"So, you're saying I was blissfully ignorant?" I questioned as my brows drew together.

"No. I'm saying you were too accepting. You should strive for more than what you can get for free, Evelyn."

"What if the free things make me happy?" I went on, heart racing. Something about how he sat there, so serious and troubled, made me want to close the distance between us and show him that happiness could be easy when you let it.

"It matters to me. I want more for you."

I shook my head, exasperated. "Why?"

"Because . . ." He paused, turmoil in his expression. A long silence elapsed, and a kaleidoscope of thoughts passed over his face, like cars going different directions on a motorway. "Because I can only see my dreams clearly when I look through you first."

My insides blared on loudspeaker, while my voice was barely a whisper. "I don't understand."

Dylan gave a sad laugh. "I just feel like any achievements are pointless unless I have you by my side."

In a heartbeat, I saw an entire life, a timeline of seventy or more years, with the only constant being Dylan's hand in mine. It was a cool idea, to have someone to share your years with, no matter where your path took you.

But what if our paths weren't one, but two?

What if I was following the yellow brick road, while he was embarking on a journey into the deep dark woods?

All these thoughts created an urgency in me. I wanted to capture this moment, drink it down like sacred water you could only ever taste once.

My body moved faster than my thoughts. I crossed the room, pulled Dylan from his seat, threw my arms around him, and kissed him like my life depended on it.

When we broke apart for air, he stared down at me, eyes glistening. "What was that for?"

"For being you," I whispered. "Even if you do make me want to pull my hair out sometimes."

I started to push him in the direction of my bedroom, but he grasped my elbows, breathing hard. "Wait, wait."

"For once in your life, Dylan, stop overthinking." I went up on my tiptoes to kiss him again. His lips welcomed mine for a brief second before he let go of me completely and backed away. He walked out into the living room, mumbling swearwords as he paced.

I frowned.

Didn't he want me?

"What's wrong?" I asked, quiet.

Dylan stood very still, his eyes on mine before he closed them. When he spoke, it all came out in a rush. "I want you, Evelyn. I want you badly. I can't count the number of times I've imagined it, but I'm not . . ." A growl. "Bloody hell."

I frowned, worried now. "You're not what?"

He grunted his frustration as he levelled his eyes on mine. "I've never done this before, okay?"

I stared at him, agape. It was the last thing I expected. I mean, a boy who looked like Dylan being a virgin was definitely rare, but then again, he wasn't your typical teenage boy. He was busy pondering the meaning of life, while other boys were out smoking joints and getting handjobs from girls in back alleyways.

My heart clenched as I looked at him, and I didn't think he could claim much more of my silly, sentimental organ, but he did.

Maybe he claimed all of it.

A flush coloured my cheeks when I replied, "Well, that makes two of us, because I've never been with anyone either."

He opened his eyes. "You haven't?"

I gave a soft laugh. "No need to sound so surprised."

He grimaced. "That's not what I meant. You're just so beautiful, and this place—"

"You're beautiful, too," I countered.

His frown formed a deep line between his eyebrows. "Men aren't beautiful, Ev."

"Yes, they are," I whispered and stepped forward. I took each of his hands in mine and gave a squeeze. "*You* are."

His eyes flickered between mine as he brought his hands up to cup my face. His voice was a whisper, "Who made you?"

I didn't have answer to that question. None of us really knew who made us, but whoever made him broke the mould.

He brought his lips to mine, kissing me carefully, gently, like I was a fragile thing that might break under too much pressure. Then his tongue slipped inside my mouth, massaging in a tender dance. I moaned, and he pushed me forward until my back hit a wall. A whump of air escaped me, but I relished the way his hands moved from my face and down my neck, over my shoulders, then down again to wrap tight around my waist.

We walked backward, never breaking the kiss, until we reached my bedroom.

Dylan pulled away to suck in a gasp of air as he urgently questioned, "Yvonne?"

"At work until late."

"You sure?"

"I'm sure. C'mere."

He came, and I kissed him more confidently than before. I felt like I knew what I was doing now. I knew his mouth. I knew he liked it when I moved my tongue along his, and when I nibbled and sucked on his bottom lip.

He lowered me onto my bed and tingles skittered along my spine at the look he gave me. It was very . . . lusty, but also full of tenderness. I lay with my head against the pillow. Breath heaving as I stared at him, I pulled my top up over my head. Dylan's gaze lowered from mine as he took in the sight of me in my bra. He mumbled something I couldn't quiet hear then came forward and gripped my hips.

He pulled me until I was flat on my back, my thighs on either side of his torso. Biting his lip, his eyes wandered over me once more. His brow was furrowed when he murmured, "Let me . . . try something."

"O-okay," I stuttered and watched as he unbuttoned my jeans.

Dylan O'Dea was unbuttoning *my* jeans.

Half of me couldn't believe this was happening, while the other half was very, very aware that it was.

When he had them off, he moved to my knickers. I noticed his hands shaking very slightly as he drew them down over my hips.

"What—"

"Please, don't say anything," he begged. "If you do I might lose my nerve."

I squeezed my lips shut, amazed by his nervousness and how tentative he was. Dylan wasn't normally a hesitant person. His throat bobbed as he swallowed and closed his eyes for a second. He slipped his fingers under the elastic of my knickers and drew them down my legs. Next, he reached under me to unclip the back of my bra.

A few seconds later I was naked under his close, attentive gaze. "You're perfect," he said, in awe. I didn't bother to correct him with all the reasons why I wasn't. I was happy to pretend. Then, a rush of anxiety flooded me, because I was completely nude. Things were getting really fucking real, but I didn't let it overwhelm me.

"Dylan."

"Hmm?" he murmured absentmindedly, his attention on my body.

"Kiss me."

"I . . . have every intention," he replied, but he still wasn't looking at my face. Instead his gaze was pinned between my legs as he pulled my thighs apart and settled his shoulders between them. He studied me like a painting on a wall, or a menu at a particularly expensive restaurant.

My pulse skyrocketed when he ran a finger down my centre, one eyebrow twitching, head tilted. Intrigue, curiosity, and stark arousal coloured his expression.

I took a mental picture for my memories, at the same time starting to hyperventilate.

"What are you—?"

My words became a sharp, surprised yelp when Dylan lowered his mouth and kissed me in my most private of places. He made a deep, raspy sound in the back of his throat. Then, capturing my gaze in his, he dragged his tongue right along my centre. It flicked at the place where the pleasure was centralized, and I let out a high-pitched whimper.

"God," I breathed.

He paused, unsure. "Am I—?"

"Don't stop."

He heeded my request and lowered his mouth to me once more. He licked and sucked, swirled his tongue around my clit until I was fisting the sheets, hips tilted upward, needing more.

His hand moved along my inner thigh, sending sparks of electricity right through me. Every touch from him, no matter how small, set my entire body alight. He groaned, like he was enjoying this just as much as I was. I squeezed my eyes shut and concentrated on what he was doing. I didn't want to miss a moment. His soft, wet tongue licking me was by far the best thing I'd ever felt in my life.

It was a flippin' miracle.

"The last time"—he breathed in between licks—"when you . . . came under me. It was the sexiest thing I've ever seen."

Funny he should mention that, because I was very close to coming again, this time on his mouth.

I trembled and clenched my thighs around him.

"I never said—"

"I know what I felt, Ev. Don't try to deny it," he countered and I shut up. He was right. There was no point denying it. He made me come from nothing but a few kisses and some carefully applied friction.

I let out a loud, erotic moan, a sound I'd never made before. It seemed to turn Dylan on even more because his licks became more aggressive. He swirled his tongue around my clit, and I felt like I'd died and gone to heaven.

Gripping his shoulders, I stared at him, unable to take my eyes off the way he worshipped me.

"You sure you've never done this before?"

"Never," he said, a sexy grin tilting his lips. "But, um, I've had a lot of mental preparation."

That meant he'd been thinking about it. Thinking about it *a lot*.

I emitted a shuddering breath as pleasure gripped me. Dylan's large hands were on my thighs, massaging me, exploring my skin, when my orgasm hit. It was swift and intense, much more so than the last time, and there were several waves of it. The first was exquisite, with each one petering out until I was no more than a sated mass beneath him.

Dylan rested his chin on my stomach and stared at me. His mouth glistened with my wetness, his hair askew. It must've been my doing, but I couldn't for the life of me remember. His mouth was like drinking a whole bottle of vodka. You blacked out, but you knew you had a bloody good time.

"I could watch you do that on repeat for the rest of my life," he said, awed. He seemed fascinated that he had the ability to make my body do things. Amazed that the stuff he'd thus far only imagined in his head actually worked in practice.

"That'd be a pretty sweet existence," I said, gazing down at him tenderly.

We remained locked in one another's gazes for a while, and Dylan seemed content to just lie between my naked legs forever.

"Not interested in moving any time soon?" I asked, playful.

He shook his head. "I think I've found my happy place."

I laughed at that. "Well, it doesn't seem fair that I'm the only one without clothes on."

He smirked. "You'll get over it."

I laughed again at his cheekiness and reached down to pull his shirt up over his head. His wide, defined shoulders were a sight to behold, but he acted like his body was nothing to brag about. He didn't seem to understand that his nakedness was just as much of a turn-on to me as mine was to him.

I was fairly sure he didn't work out, but he'd been blessed with a natural shape. He wasn't hugely muscular, but his biceps stood out, as did the cut lines of his obliques. I swept my hands over his shoulders and down his impressive back. He was perfect.

"Beautiful," I whispered.

"I told you, Ev, men aren't—"

"You're beautiful, Dylan," I said firmly, making sure he knew it was true.

He shook his head. "If you say so."

One day I'd make him believe it, but right now I just wanted to be close to him. Resting my palms flat on his chest, I ran them down his abs until they reached his belt buckle. I never broke eye contact as I carefully undid it, looking up when Dylan's breathing became erratic.

"We probably shouldn't—"

"I just want to lie here with you. We don't have to do anything."

Honestly, after the intensity of him going down on me, I wasn't sure I could handle sex. But I craved intimacy. When I went to lower his boxer shorts he grabbed my hands to stop me.

"You're eager," he said, a hint of a smile touching his lips.

I flushed, embarrassed. Was I being too forward?

Dylan must've read my thoughts when he reassured me, "Don't worry, Ev. There's nothing about any of this I don't like."

I swallowed down my self-consciousness then watched as Dylan took off his last item of clothing. I stared at him a second too long perhaps, but that was only because I'd never seen a naked boy before. Naked *man.* And his penis was erect, but that made sense, considering what we'd just been doing. I had no idea if it was big or average, but it definitely wasn't small.

I decided it was probably average, because it didn't frighten me. I imagined a large penis would be pretty scary to a first-timer. And anyway, what would I do with a huge cock? I'd need a giant vagina and . . .

Jesus, Evelyn, think about something else. Anything.

My mouth dried up, and I directed my gaze elsewhere. Turning, I went to climb under my covers. I focused on the picture of Jared Leto on my wall when Dylan climbed in and spooned me from behind. I could feel *all* of him.

He was warm and solid.

It felt like being hugged by a bear with no fur.

Okay, that was a weird thought.

Anyway.

My racing mind mimicked my racing nerves, but when Dylan placed his hand flat on my stomach and rubbed in a soothing rhythm I started to relax.

"That feels nice."

"You feel nice."

I smiled to myself and turned my head a little so I could nuzzle the underside of his jaw. His hand moved to cup my breast, and I heard a light rain patter against the window. The nuzzling quickly transformed into kissing and I sighed at the melty sensation of his body surrounding me. My eyes were closed but I was very

131

aware of his erection rubbing against the back of my thigh.

It was warm here.

And safe.

I loved kissing him.

I could kiss him forever.

If only I could.

He groaned into my mouth, and a gruff breath escaped him when he rolled us over. He grew impassioned as he settled himself between my legs and I gasped at the feel of his cock against me.

"Evelyn," he breathed, kissing my neck and moving down to my breasts.

I yelped when he circled his tongue around my nipple, tweaking the other between his fingers.

"Oh God," I cried.

"Does that feel good?"

"Yes! Don't stop."

"*Christ.*"

"Dylan."

"What do you need?"

"Make love to me."

My name was a growl on his tongue. "Ev."

He rose up and held himself above me. Breathless, he asked, "Are you sure?"

I nodded fervently. "I'm sure."

Then I dragged his mouth to mine. Our kiss was slow and languid as his hips began to move. His erection nudged at me, and I loved the hard feel of it. He started to push inside and there was a stretching sensation. His expression was agonised. I could tell he wanted to push harder, but I was too tight. I felt a sharp pain when he slowly pushed all the way in.

"*Jesus*," I gasped and gripped his shoulders.

"I'm sorry," he murmured, nibbling at my ear.

"Don't be sorry. Keep going."

"God, this feels incredible. *You* feel fucking incredible, Ev."

I was happy it felt good for him, but all I felt was sore. The pain held a pleasurable edge though, and the longer he was inside me, the more the pain faded. It was still there, but it was duller now.

I focused on his dark blue eyes, his masculine mouth and defined jaw as he moved above me. I thought about our little lives and how it took me so long to find him, even though he'd been right under my nose the whole time.

I wondered how many other people there were in the world like that. Their soulmate could be living three doors down, but the idea just never occurred to them to say hello.

I ran my fingers through his close-cropped hair. It felt soft, similar to what I imagined a cloud might feel like. My hand wandered down his neck and over the moving muscles in his back. His expression was intense, brows drawn, like he was concentrating really hard.

Concentrating on me. On us.

I think I loved him.

Something about the moment, feeling the connection between us, made me realise it was true. The words were on the tip of my tongue when Dylan let

133

out a raspy groan, his body stilling. Heat filled me and I gasped with the realisation. He'd just come.

His body fell on top of me, and he nuzzled the crook of my neck, whispering sweet things.

"You are . . . so incredible."

I closed my eyes and wrapped my arms around him. I didn't want to let him go. I knew I had to, but not yet. With that thought in my head I drifted off to sleep. When I woke up Dylan was gone. My bed felt empty and the space between my legs was sore. The faint morning light told me a long few hours had passed and Yvonne would be home. Dylan must've left before she got back though, because if she caught him I was sure I'd have been woken by the drama.

Sitting up I glanced at my bedside locker, but there was no note. I checked my phone, but there were no messages either. Nothing to show that Dylan had been here at all, except my messier than usual bed sheets.

I left my bed, took a shower, and got dressed. Some early morning gardening might help to settle my frantic mind. We lost our virginity to each other last night. It would've been nice to wake up with his arms still around me. Then again, I knew he had to leave. Yvonne sometimes came into my room to check on me when she got home from work. And like I said, if she found a boy in my bed, all hell would've broken loose.

It was a cold but bright morning when I reached the roof. No Mrs O'Flaherty or Seamus today. She was more of a mid-morning gardener and it was only six thirty. I worked for a good while before I heard footsteps approach.

When I looked up, the morning sun shone on the back of his head. It made the golden flecks in his hair glint, giving the effect of a halo. I pulled off my gloves and he smiled at me, his attention wandering from the haphazard bun atop my head, to the rumpled hoodie I wore. I'd never been much of a glam girl, not unless I was going somewhere fancy.

"Hello," I said, my voice unexpectedly hoarse. Last night had been a big deal. It had been a big deal to both of us.

"Hey," Dylan replied and came to sit beside me. He had a small paper bag in one hand and a thermos in the other. "I thought I'd find you up here."

"It's my happy place," I said, then blushed when I remembered him saying something similar last night as he lay between my thighs.

His mouth twitched ever so slightly as he set down the bag and thermos. "I brought breakfast."

I raised an eyebrow. That was sweet of him. "Oh." Twisting open the thermos, I found tea, but I gasped when I opened the bag. I glanced at him, mouth agape, "Are these—?"

He nodded. "Miracle berries. I had to traipse all the way over to the south side to find them. The only place that sells them is this fancy gourmet food market."

I smiled so wide my face hurt. "Dylan, I can't believe you did that for me."

His expression was serious. "I'd do a lot more than that for you, Ev."

Those words warmed my chest as I picked up a small red berry and placed it in my mouth.

"You need to chew it up and hold it for a minute, and make sure you spread it around with your tongue," Dylan instructed.

I did, then I pulled the wrapper off one of the sour candies he'd brought. Usually, I hated these types of sweets. My taste buds weren't fond of sour, but when I ate the candy it tasted miraculously sweet, not at all tart.

"It's so sweet. Incredible. You try one," I urged, pushing the bag at him.

Dylan ate a miracle berry, followed by a candy, smiling at me all the while. "Yep, you're right. It's a miracle," he said fondly.

"So cool. I can't wait to show Yvonne and Sam."

Dylan nodded, and we were both quiet a moment as we stared into the distance, watching the city wake up. You could see most of the Dublin skyline. The familiar buildings had always been reassuring to me. I'd never been anywhere else.

Dylan's idea of another life, a better one, nipped at the walls of my heart, working its way into my desires. What were other cities like? The people? The culture? What if all I ever knew was this one place? Would that be that enough?

I looked at him. He still gazed outward, giving me his full profile. I studied him a moment, tracing the lines of a face I adored in spite of everything.

"Dylan?" I whispered.

"Yes?" he replied, turning to face me. I wondered where his mind had been just then. Perhaps it was years ahead, in a far-off place, enjoying a life currently out of reach. Like a child eager to hear a bedtime story, I

136

wanted to know where that was, who he would be in the future. And I wanted to know if there was a place there for me.

"Tell me about your dreams."

Nine

"I want to make a difference," Dylan answered after a long moment of consideration.

"Like Mother Theresa?"

He smirked and shook his head. "No, Ev, not like Mother Theresa. Don't get me wrong, I do want to help people, but I just don't think sainthood is the way to go."

"What's the way to go then?" I asked.

"Well, first you need money, and to make it you've got to go the route of capitalism. So really, I need something I can sell. I just don't know what that thing is yet."

"You could invent a product," I suggested.

"Maybe. Or I could have someone invent one for me."

"Nah, you're far too clever not come up with something on your own."

"Being clever doesn't mean you're inventive," said Dylan. "I can sell anything to anyone though, I'm certain of that."

I smiled and glanced at my allotment. Reaching out, I plucked a jasmine flower from the plant and handed it to him. "Okay, then, sell me this."

Dylan's eyes crinkled in amusement as he took the flower. He gave it a long sniff and spun it between his fingers, pondering it a moment.

"You said one of your favourite things is the smell of jasmine in the mornings."

I nodded. "My gran taught me how to steep the flowers in water to scent a room."

"So, it's the scent that holds value, rather than the flower?"

"You could say that."

He went quiet for a second, thoughtful, then said, "What if I could capture the essence of that fresh jasmine scent? No oils or tinctures, no false replicas, just jasmine in its purest form? What if I bottled it so you never had to go to the trouble of growing the flowers, picking them, boiling the water, etc, would you buy it?"

I pursed my lips, considering it. It *was* a very lengthy process, especially when you factored in actually growing the jasmine. I guess if Dylan could create a product like that I might buy it.

"Maybe in years to come, when I have a job and don't have so much time in the mornings, sure, I'd buy it. I still love to grow the flowers though."

"But most people don't. Most people want instant gratification. And that's where I come in. I want to sell them something that gratifies them, and in the process, change my life and maybe the lives of others, too."

"How would you change other people's lives?"

"If I create a business, I create jobs. If my business is successful I might even be rich enough to give to charity, help those who don't have the resources to help themselves."

I studied him a moment, surprised by his philanthropic aspirations. I mean, I didn't think he was selfish, but I didn't know he wanted to help people in such a big way either.

"Never took you for a humanitarian," I said. In fact, he often struck me as a misanthropist, especially when he got going on a rant. But maybe he was simply expressing his dissatisfaction in humanity. Maybe he wanted to actively do his bit not to be just another arsehole among a billion other arseholes.

There were a few moments of silence as he watched me pack up my things. It was time for me to get ready for school. I imagined Dylan needed to as well, since his week-long suspension was over.

I glanced at him as we headed for the stairs. "Whatever you do end up selling, I really hope you get to achieve all those things one day."

"We only get one life, Ev. Might as well do something worthwhile with it."

I nodded as my affection for him expanded ever more. When we reached the bottom of the stairs, about to go our separate ways, Dylan caught my hand and pulled me close. Without warning, he laid a kiss on me that stole my breath. It was a tender good morning kiss, all lips and soft tongue. I smiled into it and he withdrew, smirking.

"See you at school, Ev," he said, then backed away until he turned and disappeared around the corner.

My entire body was tingling as I returned to my flat. I changed into my uniform, grabbed my school bag and coat, and headed to Sam's. His place was always a madhouse in the mornings. With five kids in a three-bedroom flat, most of them under twelve, you could understand why. Sam was the eldest, and he was often forgotten in the frenzy to take care of all the younger ones. His parents weren't bad people, but they were perennially frazzled and busy, trying to keep up with all their offspring.

"Morning Ev, come on in," his mam said when she opened the door to me. "Sam's just finishing his breakfast."

"Thanks, Pam," I replied and headed inside. Yes, Sam's mother's name was Pam. Sam and Pam. I sometimes liked to slag him off about it.

Sam sat at the kitchen table eating a bowl of cereal, while two of his younger brothers fought over a toy. His little sister brushed the hair on her Barbie doll, and the baby sat messily eating a bowl of mush.

"Hey," I said and gave a wave. His mam came in behind me and turned on the tap, filling the sink in preparation for the post-breakfast dishes.

"Maisie Feelan's young one just applied to study Business at UCD next year," she said, eyeing Sam.

Sam let out an exasperated groan. "I'm only seventeen, Ma. I don't need to apply to college until next year."

"Well, all I'm saying is, it's good to plan early. On her death bed, Granny Kennedy asked me to make sure all my children stayed in school for as long as possible. She said education is the most valuable thing you can invest in."

"I tell you what," said Sam, dropping his spoon into his now empty bowl. "Granny Kennedy was terribly talkative on her death bed. I think that's final wish number eleven we're at now, if we count brushing my teeth every night and saving myself for marriage. The woman must've never shut up when she was preparing for those pearly gates."

"Don't be cheeky," his mam chided, but there was a smile in her voice.

"Okay, well, me and Ev need to head to school now," Sam announced, getting up to grab his bag.

When we were outside, he emitted a woe-is-me sigh. "This is her new thing, nagging me about going to college. She's even been over at the Citizen's Advice, asking how to apply for grants and everything."

"Well, you're certainly clever enough," I said. "What's the big deal?"

"Ev, I barely know what I want to do with my life next week, never mind next year. She's getting way ahead of herself."

"You complain that she's always too busy with the baby and never has time for you anymore. But she's making time, and you're still complaining."

Sam tutted and folded his arms. "What has you all high and mighty this morning?"

"I just think you should appreciate her good intentions, that's all."

He eyed me closely. "Nah, that's not it. You look different. You're all, like, glowing and shit. And you seem even cheerier than usual. What's up with that?"

"Can't I just be cheery for cheeriness sake?"

"Nobody's that happy. Come on, out with it. I did note Dylan stayed behind after me and Conor left last night . . ."

I groaned. "God, I can't keep anything a secret from you."

Sam's eyes widened. "Oh em gee, Ev. What happened? Tell me everything!"

I inhaled a deep breath and whispered, "We had sex."

"What? Are you flipping serious right now? I thought you were gonna say you gave him a hand shandy or something."

I cringed. "Please don't use the phrase 'hand shandy' around me."

Sam ignored me, eager for details. "So, tell me, how was it?"

"Kinda sore. But good. I liked it."

"You just *liked* it? Wow. Dylan O'Dea is bad in bed. Who would of thought—?"

"He wasn't bad." I sighed. "It was just . . . very intense. And unexpected. I didn't think we'd go that far . . ."

"Hold up, you used protection, right?"

I bit my lip and looked away, taken off guard by his question. I'd been so swept up in the moment I hadn't thought about contraception. I mean, I was a virgin. We both were. It wasn't like we kept a stash of rubbers handy in our wallets.

"No?" I replied finally. It came out like a question and Sam gave me a slap right across the face.

"Hey! What was that for?"

"You didn't use a condom, Ev. What the hell? Do you want to end up like my mam? Or yours for that matter? Because believe me, babies might be cute to

143

look at, but all they do is poo and pee and puke all day, and poo and pee and cry all night. Is that what you want at seventeen years of age?"

"Jeez, cool your beans. I'm not pregnant." *I hope.*

"That's it. I'm frogmarching you to the GP as soon as school finishes today. We'll get you the morning after pill."

"Sam, you're overreacting."

"I am not. You're doing this, Ev. You can't get pregnant. We'll never fulfil my dreams of moving to London and sharing a swanky flat in Soho if you pop a sprog."

"A minute ago, you didn't even know what you wanted to do with your life."

"Well, us moving in together goes without saying."

I shook my head, exasperated. "Fine. We'll go to the GP if it will shut you up."

"Good. And no more unprotected sex with Dylan 'can't keep it in his pants' O'Dea. Not until I get on Amazon and buy you a year's supply of connies. I swear to God."

I couldn't help giggling at his dramatics, but when my laughter faded and reality settled in, I realised he was right. I'd gotten so caught up in Dylan that I hadn't given any thought to the consequences of having sex. Just because I was a virgin didn't mean I could be careless.

My stomach was twisted with worry all morning. Fearful thoughts ate away at me. It only subsided around lunchtime. I was making my way to the cafeteria when someone came and wrapped their arms around me from behind. I yelped in fright then turned and saw Dylan.

His smile was radiant.

"Hey," he murmured.

"Oh, hello," I said, half happy to see him, half awkward. I'd never been hugged by a boy at school before. Well yeah, I'd been hugged by Sam, but that didn't count.

"Are you going to get food?"

I bit my lip. "Uh huh."

"Can I sit with you?"

"Sure."

Sam was already in the lunchroom eating a sandwich when we went in. He was quick to give Dylan the purse-lipped, disapproving glance of an aged schoolmarm. It was very Maggie Smith.

Dylan frowned. "What are you staring at me like that for?"

Sam chewed then swallowed, his voice clipped. "No reason."

He had that tone that said there definitely *was* a reason, but Dylan didn't bite. Instead he sat and pulled out his own lunch. I did the same, and caught him watching me with a tender expression. I rolled my eyes and shook my head at him, though I was smitten by his attention. I loved the way he looked at me like I was the most interesting person in the room.

I tell you what. School days were far more exciting when Dylan O'Dea was making lovey eyes at you across the lunch table.

A minute later, Conor and Amy joined us, both in the midst of a heated discussion.

"You'll never guess what happened to Amy while she was visiting her cousins," Conor said with a grin.

Amy elbowed him in the side. "Don't you dare."

"What? You do this to me all the time, and payback's a bitch."

"Did you have sex with one of your relatives?" Sam asked. "Because I'm fairly sure that's illegal."

"Ew, no, I did not have sex with any of my cousins. Gross. They all look like Steve Buscemi."

"But if they looked like Brad Pitt you'd be all for it?" Sam continued in an attempt to rile her. I knew it by the way his lips twitched.

Amy narrowed her eyes and gave him the finger. "Fuck you, Kennedy."

"No thanks," he shot back, all sass.

"She was looking at porn on the family computer, the big dumdum," Conor revealed with a tut. "Her aunt checked the search history and narrowed it down to who was on the computer during the hours on the timestamp."

"I was bored, okay?" she said, folding her arms.

Dylan shot her a look. "Haven't you ever heard of Private Browsing?"

"Uh, no, *obviously*," Amy grumped. "If I had this never would've happened."

"Ah, good old Private Browsing," said Conor wistfully. "The most loyal member of the Armed Forces."

Dylan chuckled. "Never lets you down in a sticky situation."

"Always has your back when the time comes for a covert mission," Conor went on.

"Ugh, please, I don't want to think about either of you wanking off, thanks very much," said Amy as she shot Conor a dirty look.

I was still chuckling when a girl from Dylan's year approached. Her name was Kirsty something, and she was one of those who'd always had eyes for Dylan. In spite of his standoffishness, he still had quite the fan club among the girls at school. Kirsty could be considered one of his most ardent admirers, but I hadn't seen her attempt to talk to him since we started hanging out.

She tapped him on the shoulder and he turned, surprised to see her. A quick, lightning flash of jealousy struck my insides at the way she smiled at him.

"Hey, Dyl."

Dyl? Ugh. She might as well just call him Pickle.

Man, I was as sour as those sucking sweets I'd had for breakfast. I needed to chillax.

"Uh, hi, Kirsty."

"So, you're eighteen, right?" she asked, twisting a strand of hair around her finger.

He started to frown. "Yeah . . ."

"Me and my girls were wondering if you could buy us some alcohol this Saturday? We're having a little pre-party before we head to Godskitchen. You're welcome to join us, of course. I have a spare ticket."

147

"Ooooh, Godskitchen," Sam crooned. "What ya gonna wear? Knickers and bra?"

Seriously, it was times like these that I adored his brazenness.

Kirsty cut him a narrowed look. "I'm wearing a dress from H&M, actually."

"Good idea," Sam nodded. "Make them work for it."

"Don't you have to be eighteen to get into Godskitchen?" Amy asked. She appeared irritated by Kirsty's interruption. I knew she was the type of girl Amy vehemently disliked.

Shallow. Blonde. Wore a lot of pink.

"We have fake IDs," Kirsty replied, annoyed.

"So, forgive me if I'm being dim, but why on earth do you need *Dyl* to buy your alcohol for you?"

Conor snickered at her use of Dyl. He obviously found it amusing, too.

Kirsty's expression soured, her pretty cat eyes narrowing further. "Don't be a fucking bitch, Amy."

"I'm just pointing out the obvious."

"Yeah well, you're not helping," Kirsty hissed and let out a frustrated sigh as she looked to Dylan. "You don't need to buy us alcohol. Just come for the craic. We can, you know, do stuff." Her sultry tone shot an arrow through my temper. Was she for real right now?

I gripped the edge of the table, about to say something, when Dylan replied, "Raves aren't really my scene."

The way he said it, so dismissive, made Kirsty's chest deflate. She pressed her lips together, folded her arms and turned to leave. I heard her mutter something under her breath that sounded a lot like, "Well, I wish you'd tell someone what *is* your scene."

"Wow, that was cold, O'Dea," Sam chuckled. "Look at poor Kirsty, off to lick her wounds."

"I don't understand why she keeps trying," Amy said. "Bitch gets shut down every single time."

"Don't you know, our Dylan is quite the catch around these parts," Conor replied, smirking as he looked to me. "You should count yourself lucky, Evie."

"It's Ev, not Evie," Sam cut in. "Nobody calls her that."

Conor glanced at me, winking. "Well, I like Evie. Maybe it can be our thing."

Dylan gave him a light slap on the back of the head. "Hey. Stick to the aunt, fuckface. She's mine."

My stomach flip-flopped at those words. *She's mine*. Gone was my jealousy about Kirsty. Dylan obviously wasn't interested in her, not with the way he gazed at me across the table like I lit the flipping world up with Christmas lights. I wasn't sure I deserved such adoration, but who was I to protest?

The bell rang, signalling the end of lunch. My gut gave a pang of disappointment. My time with Dylan always seemed to be over too soon. I couldn't hang out with him after school either, because I'd promised Sam we'd go to the GP. Unfortunately, you couldn't buy the morning after pill over the counter like you could in the UK and elsewhere. You had to get a prescription first. Anyway, I didn't want to tell Dylan *that*. I was enjoying how besotted he was. There was no need to pull the curtains and let reality overshadow the stars in his eyes.

After school, Sam waited for me at reception while I went in to see the doctor.

"Evelyn Flynn?" the older woman asked as I stepped inside her office.

"Yes, hi," I replied and she looked at my details on her computer screen. I'd only been to the doctor a few times in my life, and never for anything serious. I couldn't imagine there was a whole lot there for her to be reading.

Finally, she turned and clasped her hands together. "Okay, what can I do for you today?"

I cleared my throat, suddenly embarrassed. "I need the morning after pill."

She nodded, her expression blank, as she looked at her screen again. "All right. And how long have you been sexually active?"

"Not long," I whispered.

"Can you be more specific?" she asked, all business.

"Um, I've only had sex the once."

She looked at me now, pausing momentarily, still no expression. It was unnerving. Nodding, she turned back to her screen and typed something down. "I see a lot of girls from St. Mary's here. They don't usually wait so long."

On the surface, her words were benign, but the insult beneath was clear. Her disdain for people where I lived was obvious, and I took offence. We weren't all reckless, sex-crazed teens having babies before our

150

time. Some of us fell in love with boys who spoke about the human condition like it fascinated him endlessly. Boys who aspired to achieve things far beyond the reach of our perceivably low existence.

I hated that this woman thought we were all louts, happy to live on social welfare and sponge off the government, because it wasn't true. Sure, that did describe a lot of people, but it didn't describe the ones I held dear, like Yvonne and Sam and Dylan. Even Conor and Amy had worked their way into my affections a little. We weren't a bunch of numbers on a computer screen. We were real people with hearts and souls and feelings. But I guess those above preferred to stereotype and disregard those below. It was easier than having to emote. Easier than making the effort to *understand*.

"I'm glad my patience impresses you," I said, eyeing the doctor coolly. My cold voice, along with my carefully collected expression seemed to surprise her.

She backtracked a little. "I didn't mean to insult you."

"Of course not," I replied, while my tone said *yes, you did.* She just didn't think I'd bite back.

More and more I was starting to agree with Dylan's view of the world. He hated when people figured out where he came from and looked down on him for it. Well, I now realised I hated it, too.

I walked out of the office with the prescription I'd come for, but my mood was nowhere near as cheerful as when I'd arrived. It soured further when Sam and I walked into the pharmacy down the street and Kirsty stood in the cosmetics section. She was with two of her girlfriends, and they appeared to be browsing the fake tanning options.

Probably stocking up for Godskitchen, I thought bitterly.

Bitterness wasn't a normal reaction for me, but when it came to Dylan, I was feeling all sorts of new emotions. I was possessive of him, felt like he was mine, just the same as he claimed me to be his.

Keeping my chin up, I walked to the pharmacist's counter and handed over my prescription. Sam was preoccupied with a text on his phone and hadn't yet noticed Kirsty and Co. I waited while the girl went to fill my prescription, nervously biting on my fingernails. I didn't want Kirsty to see what I was getting.

Unfortunately, my worst fears came true when Sam and I made to leave and she spotted us. Quick as a flash she sauntered over. She wasn't too much taller than me, but I was still intimidated.

"Getting your monthly AIDS medication, is it?" she asked snidely and her friends snickered.

I decided to stay quiet, not bothering to reply to her insult. Sam, however, wasn't much of a pacifist, because he cut her a scathing look.

"Don't presume everyone's as riddled as you are, Kirsty. Heard you got the clap from Danny Doolan last summer."

Kirsty tensed. "Who told you that?"

Sam barked a laugh. "Nobody had to tell me. The rumour's all over school."

I swear to God, Sam needed to consider getting into acting, because he really could sell a lie. Kirsty looked to her friends.

"Did either of you hear anything about this?"

They both wore identical dumb expressions as they shook their heads.

"I'm going to *kill* Danny when I get my hands on him. He's always telling people we shagged."

With that she dropped the bottle of fake tan and stormed out of the pharmacy.

"Oh my God, I love you," I said, giggling as Sam threw his arm around my shoulder.

"Nobody talks to my Ev like that and gets away with it."

I smiled wide and gave him a peck on the cheek. "Seriously, I don't know what I'd ever do without you."

Ten

Arnotts wasn't a department store I visited often. Yvonne and I sometimes went there when we did our Christmas shopping, but mostly to browse. After casting our covetous gazes on designer handbags, overpriced dresses and winter coats we could never afford, we'd head across the street to buy much more inexpensive versions in Penneys.

When I called on Dylan this morning, his dad told me he was at work, and I remembered his weekend job. Since I needed to go into town to run some errands for Yvonne, I thought I'd drop by and catch him on his break.

I wandered past various counters in search of him and was stopped a number of times by sales people trying to peddle their wares.

When I finally spotted Dylan, I paused and admired him for a second. He wore a crisp black shirt, matching slacks, and a name tag. His sandy hair stood out against the dark colours as he smiled politely at a woman who stood by his counter. She looked to be in her fifties and already carried several shopping bags in hand.

Dylan lifted a bottle of perfume to show her. "This one is quite elegant, I think. It has a powdery, musky scent that makes a statement. But if you want to go lighter," he said, placing the bottle down and lifting another, "I'd recommend this one. It's sweeter, mildly floral."

The way he spoke was different. He still sounded the same, but his accent was subtler. I wondered if he did it on purpose to make shoppers feel more at ease, or if it was like a telephone voice, where you didn't realise you were doing it.

"I'm quite fond of orange scents. Do have anything citrusy?" the woman asked. This was fascinating, watching Dylan at work. He appeared so relaxed behind that counter, so confident, like he was ready to answer any question, fulfil any request. He reminded me of a sexy concierge in a period drama.

"Hmm, let me see," he said, perusing the shelf next to him. He plucked a bottle and pulled off the cap. "I think you might like this one. It gives a burst of bergamot and zingy lemon that is quite intoxicating." He took each perfume and spritzed a single spray of each on a thin strip of card.

"Here, try them all and see which you prefer."

The woman smiled in the way a mother might smile at her son for doing well on a school test. "You have a way with words, young man," she said, taking her time to sniff each card. "The girl who works at this counter during the week isn't half as descriptive as you."

"I have a very acute sense of smell," Dylan replied, then gave a self-deprecating smile. "And too big a vocabulary, or so my dad says. Helps me win arguments."

"I can imagine his annoyance," said the woman with a laugh. "I'll take this one." She handed him the third strip of card, the citrusy one.

"Very good choice," said Dylan as he went to retrieve the boxed and sealed bottle of perfume. He rang up the purchase and the woman went happily on her way. It was only then that I approached.

"So," I said, glancing at his name tag like we were strangers. "What else can you do with that acute sense of smell, Mr O'Dea?" My tone was flirtatious, and Dylan smiled fondly. I was so glad he looked pleased to see me.

"Many things. What are you doing here?"

"I called to your flat, but your dad said you were working. I had to come into town anyway, so"—I spread out my arms—"here I am."

Dylan's eyes warmed. "Here you are." He lowered his voice as he cast his gaze around to make sure no one was looking. "C'mere."

I stepped forward and he briefly caught my jaw in his palm, pulling my mouth in for a quick kiss before he let go. A girl on the counter opposite Dylan's smirked, then pretended to focus on the small cosmetics boxes she was sorting.

Dylan stepped back and cleared his throat. "Well, now that you're here, I can finally do something I've wanted to for as long as I can remember."

My brows rose. "Oh?"

"I want to pick you out a perfume."

A glimmer of excitement ran through me, then disappointment as I replied, "I can't afford anything."

"I'm buying," Dylan assured me. I was about to protest when he lifted a finger to shush me. "I get a staff discount."

"I bet everything still costs a bomb, even with the discount."

"You let me worry about that," he said and took my hand to pull me closer. "I've selected perfumes for countless women, and you're the only one I've fantasised doing it for. Let me enjoy this."

Well, that was . . . well. I felt a little breathless as a swell of anticipation filled me. I watched him pick out a selection of bottles off a glass shelf.

"How do you make your selections?" I asked, intrigued.

Dylan scratched his jaw, glancing at me intently. "Your skin has a scent. Everybody's does. It's a bit like how everyone's house smells a certain way. It's representative of the life you live. Each person's skin gives off an odour, and the right fragrance for that person depends on that odour. All of these"—he gestured to the sample bottles—"are perfect for yours."

He noticed how my skin smells? The idea sent a shiver down my spine, a pleasant one. Although it wasn't so surprising considering how up close and personal he'd been with it. But then, he said he'd been thinking about this a long time, that meant well before we really knew each other. He definitely couldn't have known how I smelled back then.

I scanned the brands: Chanel, Gucci, Versace, Chloé, Yves Saint Laurent. The names were synonymous with luxury, silk dresses, designer shoes, and town cars. They weren't me. Not at all.

"I'm much more of a Body Shop sort of girl."

157

"Nothing wrong with the Body Shop," said Dylan. "What's your favourite perfume there?"

I shrugged. "Yvonne usually gets me a bottle of White Musk for my birthday. I like it, but I didn't pick it out myself. I've never really given too much thought to perfume."

Dylan made a humming noise, like he was thinking about something. "I smell that on you sometimes," he said, not looking at me while he considered the bottles. My stomach did a tiny flip.

"Musk is a good place to start," he went on, selecting the bottle of *Gucci* by Gucci. He spritzed it on a strip of paper, just like he'd done for his last customer, then handed it to me.

I sniffed it and wrinkled my nose. "That's way too strong."

Dylan's mouth twitched. "I thought you might say that."

"It smells like something an eighty-year-old woman would wear, and mostly because her sense of smell is failing her."

Dylan chuckled and I narrowed my gaze at him. "You knew I wasn't going to like that one, didn't you?"

"Just wanted to test a theory."

"Of?" I probed.

"Whether or not I've guessed your preferences accurately based on the things you surround yourself with. You say you've never given much thought to perfume, but your life is full of scent, Ev. All the plants you devote your time to, they give off their own little signatures all around you."

I furrowed my brow. "Really?"

"Try this one," he said, ignoring my question as he handed me a tester bottle of Versace 'Bright Crystal'. "It's flowery and fruity, with a base note of musk."

I sprayed some on a piece of card and took a whiff. "Hmm, I like it, but I don't love it."

Dylan took the bottle from me and replaced it with another. "Next one."

I read the label aloud. "Chloé. This one looks familiar." I inhaled. "Smells like roses."

"That's one of the middle notes," said Dylan. "What do you think?"

"It's . . . nice."

He narrowed his gaze playfully. "You're a hard one to please, Miss Flynn."

"What can I say? I have high standards."

Dylan gave an indulgent smile. "Okay, try this. It just came out this year. It's an oriental."

The bottle read 'Flowerbomb' by Viktor Rolf. I shot Dylan a curious look. "What's an oriental?"

He folded his arms as he explained, "So, there are eight main categories of perfume. You've got citrus, floral, fruity, green, oceanic, spicy and oriental. Orientals are musky and sensual. They give an air of mystery."

I shot him a smirk as I inhaled. "It's so strange that you know all this."

He shrugged. "It's my job."

"I bet half the people who work fragrance counters in this store don't know a third of what you do."

"Well, let's say I'm strangely obsessed then."

I grinned and handed him back the bottle. "Let's. Also, I really like that one. It's definitely my favourite."

"Then it's yours."

"But it's so expensive," I protested, even though I really loved the idea of owning something so special. It smelled like bergamot and green tea, with a hint of jasmine and orchids. There was musk in there, too. I felt like wearing it would make me feel more confident somehow, which was ridiculous because it was only a scent. How could a scent give you confidence? Yet another thing I'd argued with Dylan over, and again, it turned out he was right.

"Good," he said fondly. "You deserve expensive things."

I flushed at that and glanced at my hands. Where had this boy come from? He exploded into my life with his kindness and romantic sentiments and unsolicited gifts.

"I've been meaning to tell you, it's Conor's birthday tomorrow," Dylan went on as he slotted the box of perfume into a bag. "We're going out tonight to celebrate. You should come."

I let out a sigh. "I'd love to, but I'm not eighteen. I won't get in anywhere."

He frowned. "I keep forgetting that."

Disappointment filled me, because I hadn't spent time with him all this week and a night out would've been perfect. As I thought about it, an idea struck.

"Hey, if Conor and Amy are up for it, why don't you all come to The Morgan? That's where Yvonne works. I could convince her to let us have the roof bar

160

for an hour or two if I promise not to drink any alcohol."

Dylan seemed interested. "Well, I know Conor would love it. Do you think she'll agree?"

I grinned at him. "Who could say no to this face?"

He smiled then his expression heated as he quietly replied, "I know I can't."

He silently handed me the bag and I backed away from the counter, mostly because I was in danger of kissing him very impolitely if I didn't.

"I'll call later and let you know the verdict."

"Talk to you then, Evelyn."

Eleven

Yvonne said yes to the party.

I think it was mostly because she had a soft spot for Conor after our unexpected get together the other week. When he revealed his insecurities, she'd warmed to him in a maternal way.

She was completely oblivious to his crush.

Maybe she never had to know. After all, I was fairly certain Conor wouldn't be brave enough to ever tell her. He'd soon find some other girl to fancy and forget all about my aunt.

I wore a forest-green skirt and a black lace top with some ballet flats for the night. Sam came over to get ready in my room, but he was distracted.

"Any more developments with Shane?"

Sam shook his head, though his expression was cagey. "He hasn't come near me at all. I think the kiss freaked him out."

"Well, maybe it's for the best. Boys like him only cause trouble."

"Yep. That's why I'm keeping my distance," Sam agreed, but I got a sense he only said it to keep me happy.

I exhaled and spritzed on some of the perfume Dylan gifted me. I breathed in, savouring the musky richness.

"Oooh, that looks fancy," Sam commented as he plucked the bottle from me to read the label. He let out a low whistle. "Where'd you get the money for this?"

I snatched it back. "I didn't. It was a gift from Dylan."

"It must be serious if he's buying you perfume."

"Maybe."

"Oh, quit pretending you're not delighted."

"I will when you quit pretending you're not intrigued by Shane."

Sam huffed and folded his arms. "Whatever."

"You can deny it all you want, but I know you're flattered by him kissing you."

"Fine. We're both a pair of smug Susans. Now come on, we need to get to The Morgan before the others arrive."

I knew he was changing the subject, but I let him, because we really did need to leave if we didn't want to be late. Yvonne met us at the door then escorted us to the roof herself.

"Okay, you have two hours, but I'll be up periodically, so don't think you can sneak any drinks. There are plenty non-alcoholic options," she warned before heading downstairs.

I took a seat at the table and poured us each a Coke. "Looks like the only high we'll be getting tonight is a sugar one," I joked.

Sam shot me a look. "Eff that, I'm having a vodka."

"Well, don't say I didn't warn you. It'll be you who has to face Yvonne's wrath when she finds out."

He grinned and screwed open a bottle to take a quick swig. "*Sooo* worth it."

My phone pinged with a text from Dylan to say he and the others had arrived. My stomach tightened and excitement fizzled through me. I couldn't wait to see him. When the three of them came through the door, Sam and I jumped up and shouted a chorus of, "SURPRISE!"

"Oh my God, so cool," Conor exclaimed as he looked around.

"Do we have this whole place to ourselves?" Amy asked, camcorder going as she captured a three-sixty of the rooftop. For once, she actually seemed impressed.

I smiled wide. "Yep. For two whole hours. Grab yourselves a drink."

Dylan's eyes wandered appreciatively over my body as he approached then dipped down to press a kiss on my lips. He inhaled and whispered in my ear, "You're wearing it."

I nodded shyly. "Yep."

"It suits you. You have good taste."

I poked his shoulder. "You're the one who picked it out."

"Right, then I have good taste." He smirked and rested his hand on the small of my back as we joined the others at the table. I enjoyed the warmth of his palm, and tried not to fixate on where I wanted the night to end. I had missed his touch, his taste.

"So, what have you three been up to this week?" Sam asked. "Any gossip?"

He eyed Dylan in particular, and I could've murdered him. I knew he was referring to us having sex. Sam was aware I'd been a virgin, but he didn't know Dylan was, too. He would've had a field day with that piece of info.

"Same old, same old," Conor muttered.

"My neighbour's cat died," Amy told us. "She's battling with the council, because they won't let her bury it outside the flats. The morbid twist is, it's been dead a week, and she's got it bagged up and chilling in her freezer until she can find an acceptable burial place."

"Ew! A dead cat right next to the *Birdseye* chicken nuggets." Sam made a face.

"Why doesn't she just have it stuffed? My dad used to be friends with this bloke who did taxidermy on the weekends. His shed was full of dead animals," Dylan said.

"Now that's even creepier." Conor shuddered. "Little Fluffy sitting on your mantelpiece forevermore. Watching you. *Always* watching."

"I don't mind stuffing animals. It's just the idea of her keeping it in the freezer that freaks me out. Puts me right off my food every time I think about it."

"I thought you'd be all into that sort of thing," Sam commented.

"What? Because all goths love dead things?" she asked derisively. "I dress this way because it's fucking cool, not because I think I'm a vampire or a zombie or some shit."

"Fair enough," Sam replied, hands in the air as he looked to Dylan again. "So, no news on your front?"

He slowly shook his head. "Nothing that springs to mind."

"You sure? You didn't make any unwise, spontaneous decisions that could change a young girl's life forever?"

"Sam!" I hissed.

"What? He needs a talking to, and I'm the only one prepared to give it."

I closed my eyes and buried my head in Dylan's shoulder, mortified. "I'm so sorry about him," I mumbled into his shirt.

"Still not ringing any bells?" Sam continued. "Well, I'll spell it out for you. Next time, wear a rubber. We don't want any little Dylalyns running around with nappies that need changing."

That was it. As soon as I got Sam alone he was going to SUFFER. The ALL CAPS variety.

Dylan sounded amused. "Dylalyns?"

"It's what your unwanted baby would be called. You know, like Brangelina?"

Dylan turned his head to whisper in my ear. "You told him?"

I nodded. "I'm sorry."

"Don't be," he went on, still whispering. "And I would've used protection only I didn't exactly plan for it to happen."

"No, I know that. He's just making a big deal out of—"

"I can hear you both, you know," Sam cut in. "And it's not nothing."

"Hold up a second, you two had *sex*?" Conor asked.

"If you ask me, it was obvious," Amy added, unimpressed. "I mean, look at them. You can practically smell the pheromones."

"It's nobody's business but ours," I said. "So, you can all talk about something else."

"Great. Now I'm the only one who's still a virgin," Conor grumped.

Sam gasped, his eyes on Dylan. "*You* were a virgin."

Dylan shrugged, like it was no big deal.

"But how? What about all the Kirstys at school fighting to get into your britches?"

"Nobody uses the word 'britches' anymore," Amy interjected.

"Well, I do," Sam countered, still taken aback. "I can't believe it."

"Like I said, it's not your business," I repeated then glanced at Conor. "And don't worry. You're not the only virgin among us. Sam's still as untouched as freshly fallen snow."

"*Evelyn*," Sam shrieked.

Conor chuckled. "Yay, now I feel less alone."

Sam harrumphed and folded his arms, shooting me an irritable look as he pulled out his phone to check his messages. He proceeded to ignore everyone for the next half hour. I felt a little bad for outing him, but after embarrassing me in front of Dylan, he deserved it.

167

I'd just finished my second Coke when I leaned across to look at the screen of his phone. He was so absorbed in his text conversation that he didn't even notice me reading over his shoulder.

Shane: Where u at?

Sam: Having drinks on the roof of The Morgan :-P

Shane: Living it large, eh? Me 2. I've been on the lash since yesterday.

Sam: Thought you might be on a continual sesh.

Shane: Why's that?

Sam: Because you only ever text me when you're shitfaced.

Sam: And haven't been home in days.

Sam: And using poor judgement.

Shane: Fuck you.

Sam: Bye Shane.

He turned off his phone and I stiffened. I couldn't believe he had Shane's number. And it seemed like they'd been texting regularly.

"Sam," I said, and he jumped, emitting a tiny gasp. "Were you just reading—?"

"You're texting Shane," I whisper-hissed, and his mouth formed a thin line.

"If you and Dylan are none of my business, then me and Shane are none of yours."

"Yes, but—"

"I mean it, Ev," he gritted. His jaw was tight so I knew he was serious.

I stared at him for a long moment, and I couldn't deny that my feelings were hurt. Things had obviously been transpiring between him and Shane, and I'd been privy to none of it. When he saw my sad expression, he let out a sigh and gave my hand a squeeze.

"Look, I just turned off my phone. I'm done with him. I'm not gonna be his dirty little secret."

I studied him, trying to figure out if he was telling the truth. "Promise?"

He squeezed my hand tighter. "I promise."

"Hey, you lot. How's everything going up here?" came Yvonne's voice as she stepped onto the roof. Conor smiled wide when he saw her.

"Great. Thanks so much for letting us up here," he said.

"Oh, no worries. And happy birthday," she replied as she approached to give him a hug. Yvonne had always been a hugger, but she was unaware of how much the gesture meant to Conor. He looked like all his Christmases had come at once as she wrapped her arms around his shoulders and gave a squeeze.

When she pulled back, her attention went to the drinks in front of Sam and me. We both had glasses of Coke, but while mine was unsullied, Sam's was laced with vodka. I think she might've suspected as much, but she didn't comment on it.

"Well, how are the celebrations going?"

"Great," Amy enthused. She was a lot friendlier when she was drunk, and she'd already had a few. "This is an amazing spot. I can't believe I never knew about it."

Yvonne smiled. "It's a hidden gem all right. Can I get you guys anything? Want any peanuts or scampi fries from down at the bar?"

"Yes," I said. "If it's not too much trouble."

"Not at all, hon." She leaned over to give me a quick kiss on the temple. "I'll be right back. I'm on my break for the next half hour."

As soon as she was gone Conor looked around like he was on cloud nine. "She hugged me."

"Yep. Better store the memory for tonight's wet dream," Amy teased.

"Nothing you say can ruin this for me, Amy. This is the best birthday ever."

"Even better than that time your dad took us bowling?" Dylan asked with a grin.

"I think this just about trumps that," Conor said sarcastically just as the door to the roof opened again. I was about to praise Yvonne for her speediness but then saw it wasn't her.

It was Shane.

If you looked up the definition of drunk in the dictionary, you'd find a picture of him.

Sam immediately stood and hurried over. "What are you doing here?" he asked, frazzled. Shane didn't answer, but instead grabbed Sam and kissed him right on the mouth. He looked like he was trying to eat his face, if I was being honest.

"Oh . . . my . . . God," Amy breathed, slack-jawed.

"Look at that butt," Conor added tipsily. She scowled at him, and he apologised. "Sorry, couldn't help myself."

Sam was glued to the spot, too shocked by Shane's sudden appearance to react right away.

"Should we . . . do something?" Dylan asked. He and I were the only two not intoxicated at this point.

"Don't," Amy hissed. "I want to see what happens next."

"She's right," Conor added. "It's like a soap opera."

Finally, Sam gripped Shane's shoulders and pushed him away. He sucked in a breath and whispered, "You need to leave." For once in his life, he actually appeared embarrassed.

"But I wanted to see you," Shane whined. He didn't seem like his normal self at all. He was drunk and bleary eyed. Even his voice was less harsh. Maybe this was more of the real Shane than the bully who threw his weight around at school.

"Well, I don't want to see you," Sam replied and folded his arms across his chest.

Shane came closer and caught one of Sam's hands in his. "Please, Sam. Just give me five minutes."

Sam glanced at me, and I could see how conflicted he was. My eyes begged him not to give in, but he did anyway. "Okay, five minutes," he sighed. "We can go downstairs."

I was about to stand up and tell him not to go, but Dylan grabbed my arm. "Let him fight his own battles," he murmured quietly.

"But I don't want to. He's my best friend."

"You're not his protector. He's stronger than you think."

Was he though? Despite all his big talk, my little Sam was so diminutive and sensitive when it came down to it. He was a gentle soul. And gentle souls shouldn't try to find their match in hard ones. They only got crushed in the end.

The door closed behind them, and I grew anxious. Every second I wanted to get up and follow, but I knew Dylan was right. Sam wouldn't thank me for meddling. The last time I did all I achieved was a punch in the face.

Dylan wrapped his arm around my shoulders. "He'll be okay. And if he isn't I'll give Shane a hiding."

I mustered a smile. "My hero."

He circled my wrist with his fingers. His thumb brushed against the inside and a quiver ran through me. He made a low hum in the back of his throat before he pondered, "How shall I help you relax?"

The low, quiet way he spoke made my tummy flutter. I blinked a few times then pressed a soft, unsure kiss to his lips. "Kissing is good."

"It is. If only your aunt wasn't coming back up in a minute."

"If only," I sighed then settled into him. I liked the feel of his body at my side.

When Yvonne returned, her arms were full of salty snacks. She dropped them all on the table and announced, "Dig in. I don't consider my job done unless your cholesterol has risen a few points before the night is through."

I laughed and opened up a packet of peanuts.

Yvonne's brows furrowed as she looked around. "Where'd Sam go?"

"His friend turned up. He'll be back in a little bit," I replied, not getting into the fact that it was Shane. My aunt was even more protective of Sam than I was. If I was her adoptive daughter, he was her adoptive son.

She sat between Conor and Amy, and Conor seemed content to just gaze at her longingly.

"So, another birthday bites the dust, eh?" she said and took a sip from the glass of orange juice she'd brought up. "Tell us, what are your hopes for the next year?"

Yvonne was all about the hopes and dreams. And she loved people who were like her, people who aspired to more than what they were handed. I was sure she'd approve of Dylan's aspirations for a better life.

"Getting into college will be good enough for me," Conor replied. "At the very least it'll keep my parents happy."

"Oh, but you must want more than that," Yvonne chided. "A girlfriend, maybe? Perhaps to meet your idol?"

Conor knocked back a long gulp of beer. I could see his tipsiness gave him courage to converse with Yvonne. "I don't really have any idols, but a girlfriend would be nice." He flashed her a sheepish grin. "You're single, right?"

Yvonne chuckled and smacked him on the shoulder. "Oh, you sweet talker." She thought he was joking, which was funny because we all knew he wasn't. "I'm sure Ev might have a few friends at school she could introduce you to."

I shot her a look. "You know Sam is my only friend, and I'm pretty sure Conor isn't interested."

"Well, what about Amy here? She's your friend, isn't she?" Yvonne went on.

Amy and I exchanged a glance. Technically, we were friends, but we'd never really spent any time alone together. "Well, yes, but—"

Amy held up a hand to stop me. "I'm not a candidate. Going out with Conor would be like dating my brother."

"Hey! I'm not that bad."

She arched a brow. "*Do* you want to go out with me?"

"I see your point."

"Just out of curiosity, are there any boys at school you're interested in?" I inquired.

"I'd do Owen Costello, and Eddie Ryan's not bad-looking. Other than that, no. They're all vile."

Both of the boys she mentioned were lone wolf types, a little like Dylan, actually. I wondered why she never thought to fancy him. Then again, they'd been friends since they were little. Maybe it'd just feel too weird to like someone you'd known that long.

"Eddie Ryan sits next to me in Biology," I said. "I could put in a good word for you."

Amy shifted closer. "Now we're talking. What'll you say?"

"I could ask him if he has a girlfriend."

"Don't do that." Dylan frowned. "He'll think you're asking for yourself."

"No, he won't. Boys at school aren't interested in me."

Dylan gave a disbelieving laugh. "You're funny, Evelyn. *Hilarious*."

"Yeah," Amy added. "Everybody thinks you're gorgeous. It's annoying."

"If that's the case, then why don't I ever get asked out?" I countered.

"Because if they did I'd kill them," Dylan shot back, his arm around my waist now. It was a little too intimate for my liking, given that Yvonne was sitting right there talking to Conor. I shifted in place, but he didn't lessen his hold.

"Well, anyway, I'm fairly sure Eddie Ryan isn't interested in me, so I can do some matchmaking for Amy. I'll talk to him on Monday and let you know how it goes at lunch."

"Tell him I'll meet him in the toilets for a quickie."

"Amy," Dylan admonished. "You will not—"

"I'm joking. Just tell him, I don't know, that I think he's hot and see what he says."

"I may have to rephrase it slightly, but I'll do my best."

"I don't like this," Dylan grumped.

I furrowed my brow. "Why?"

"Because you're my girlfriend, that's why."

That shut me right up, and my heart raced. We hadn't made things official, not yet. I suspected in Dylan's head us being an item went without saying. My mouth ran dry as I stared at him. I also wondered if

Yvonne had heard, but when I glanced across the table she and Conor were deep in conversation.

"Well, yes," I replied shakily. "But that doesn't mean I can't play matchmaker for Amy." I tried to be cool, but it was hard when his words kept running through my head in a loop.

You're my girlfriend.

You're my girlfriend.

You're my girlfriend.

"Fine," he allowed. "But if he tries coming onto you, I'll give him a hiding."

"Jaysus, you're in the mood to give half of Dublin a hiding tonight," Amy commented wryly. Dylan flipped her off just as Yvonne let out a squeak of surprise.

I looked over just in time to see Conor try to kiss her. She leapt up from her seat like it was on fire. "Oh no, honey, that's not what I—"

"I didn't mean it. I was only joking," Conor replied lamely.

Not one to prolong anyone's embarrassment, my aunt sucked in a quick breath and pulled herself together. "Right well, I need to be getting back to the bar. You lot enjoy the rest of your party, and Ev, I'll see you at the flat later."

With that she turned and hurried out the door. Sam was returning as she left, but she was too flustered to stop and talk to him. He stared at her retreating figure then looked to the rest of us. His hair was askew, his clothes rumpled, and his lips raw. Obviously, he and Shane had some sort of fumble, and my chest burned for him.

Oh Sam, what are you doing?

"Okay, that was weird. What did I miss?"

Conor stared at the ground while Dylan, Amy, and I struggled for the right words to explain his awkward, mortifying attempt to kiss my aunt. Instead of making him suffer, I decided to be merciful and change the subject.

"Nothing. Now come over and help me finish these Cokes before our time here runs out. You've been gone too long."

Twelve

Dylan had to work all day Sunday.

On Monday, I didn't expect to see him until lunch, but he surprised me by showing up at my flat before school. Yvonne was still fast asleep, having worked a late shift the night before. I let him in with a smile and went up on my tiptoes to give him a kiss.

"Missed you," I whispered.

I'd only meant for it to be a quick peck, but Dylan closed his eyes, his mouth practically sinking into mine. He quietly groaned and deepened the kiss by sliding his tongue past my lips. I gasped at the unexpected but pleasant intrusion. He wrapped his arms around my middle and walked me backwards to my bedroom.

"What are you doing?" I asked, breaking away long enough to ask the question. Yvonne could wake up and hear him. Then I'd have to explain why I had a boy in my room at eight a.m.

"I've gone a whole week without you," he rasped, like that was explanation enough. His hands fumbled at the waist of my uniform.

"We have to go to school," I protested.

"You'll get there on time. I promise," he said then put his mouth on my neck. That was when my brain stopped working. When he touched me, I was helpless; I let him do whatever he wanted. He laid me flat on my bed, divested my entire lower half of clothing, then went to town on me with his lips, teeth, and tongue. It was torture not to make a sound as my gasps and laboured breaths filled the room.

Dylan looked sexy and ruffled in his uniform, his eyes on mine as he dragged his tongue over my clit in a lazy, repetitive rhythm. It felt like there were a dozen tiny explosions going off inside me. I fisted my duvet, back arching as my orgasm built.

Dylan palmed my hips, his gaze dark as he drove me to the heights of pleasure. I wanted to scream, but I couldn't. I wanted to tear his clothes off and pull him on top of me, but we didn't have time.

When I came, my entire body convulsed. Dylan licked at me until I was completely sated, like he couldn't get enough.

"Pretty," he murmured as I tried to catch my breath.

"Uh . . . thanks," I replied shyly.

"We should start every day exactly like this," he went on and I gave a soft laugh.

"You'll hear no complaints from me."

Was this what it would be like? If we moved away together? I felt incredible, like nothing bad could touch me, but I also felt guilty, because I wanted more. I wanted Dylan on top of me, inside me, under me. I just *wanted.* I wanted him to know the pleasure he just gave me.

He exhaled a frustrated breath, then pulled me up from the mattress. "Come on, I better get you to school if I'm going to keep my promise."

On the way to our first class, we had to walk by Kirsty and her friends. Dylan held my hand the entire way, and for the first time I felt like we were a real

179

couple. We were showing the world it was official, and I liked that, but I hated the attention. Kirsty's gazed slithered along our linked fingers, and I caught a micro-expression of irritation.

Oh, well.

I suppose I better get used to being hated by Dylan's bevvy of admirers.

We stopped outside my classroom, and he gave me a quick kiss on the lips. "See you at lunch, Ev."

"Yeah, see you then," I replied.

All through my morning classes, I could smell him on me, a heady mix of his cologne and something that was just him. He was right. Each person did have their own scent, and Dylan's was my favourite. I couldn't stop thinking about him coming over to the flat just to go down on me. I was basically in my own little world. I took nothing in during class as I relived the whole thing all morning.

That was probably why I didn't see Kirsty follow me into the bathroom, although I did get an odd feeling on the back of my neck. My hairs stood on end, like my body sensed a threat my brain was too slow to pick up on.

I stood by the sink, washing my hands then looked up. Kirsty and several of her friends were watching me, and those hairs stood up even further. I was outnumbered. She eyeballed me as she chewed on a piece of gum, then slowly pulled it out of her mouth. Without a word, she stepped forward and mashed it into the back of my head.

"What the hell?" I exclaimed and turned around to face her.

"Stay away from Dylan."

"Or what? You'll put more gum in my hair? You're disgusting."

She smirked and started to back away. "Good luck getting it out, slut."

Her friends snickered and followed her out, while I tried to contain my rapidly growing temper. I wasn't one to lose my cool, but then again, nothing like this had ever happened to me before. I was too bland a target for bullying. I blended into the background. But not anymore. Not with Dylan O'Dea as my boyfriend.

I tried to pull the gum from my hair with some tissue, but it only made matters worse. I needed help. Sliding my phone from my pocket, I quickly sent Sam an SOS. He showed up minutes later, arching a *what the fuck are you looking at?* brow at a student who glared at him for being in the girls' bathroom.

"Oh my God, that little bitch," he said on a gasp when he saw my hair.

"Is it really bad?" I asked, unable to see the full extent of the damage.

"It's bad, but fixable. She's just a jealous cow. That's why she did it."

"I know that. I just hate this sort of thing. You know I'm a pacifist."

Sam grinned. "Yeah, unless you're defending me. Then you're a crazy mofo who'd claw somebody's eyes out."

181

"Well, yeah," I allowed. "But that's a special circumstance."

"Okay, I think we may have to tie it up until we get home. If we rub some peanut butter, or maybe a spoonful of vegetable oil in, it'll come out nicely."

"Ugh," I groaned. "Kirsty's saliva is gonna be in my hair all day."

"I know, but there's nothing else for it. I promise I'll get this gunk out as soon as we get home."

"You're a lifesaver," I said, thanking him.

"Come on, let's go have something to eat before lunch is over."

I nodded and followed him out. On our way to the cafeteria, we passed by Shane. Unlike usual, he wasn't scowling at Sam, but grinning. However, much like usual, he threw an insult at him.

"Hey fag."

"Hey dickface," Sam shot back.

"Suck any cocks today?" Shane retorted.

"Why? You interested?" Sam asked back and Shane grinned wider as he continued down the hall.

"Okay, that was . . . bizarre."

"I discovered it's best to play him at his own game. Actually, I think he likes it."

I arched a brow. "What? Like a sadist who enjoys victims that fight back?"

Sam made a face like he was thinking about it. "Hmm, maybe."

"It's weird."

"You think I don't know that? Every time I promise myself I'm not going to talk to him anymore, I'm

182

replying to his texts five minutes later. There's something seriously wrong with me."

"No, there isn't. You're just enjoying having someone be interested in you. It's not your fault your admirer is incapable of normal, healthy interactions. Is that how he talks to you all the time?"

Sam shook his head. "Only when other people are around."

"And when you're alone?"

He chewed on his lip. "When we're alone we don't do much talking."

"So, it's all . . . sexual?" I whispered.

"Basically."

"Have you had sex with him?"

"Not yet."

"That means you're going to."

"No, it doesn't. But even if I do, you don't need to worry. I don't have feelings for him. I just like this whole secret tryst we have going on. It's exciting."

I studied him worriedly. Sam might've convinced himself he hadn't developed feelings, but I wasn't so sure. I'd been smitten with Dylan before we kissed. Before we had sex. But once he'd touched my body, kissed me, every feeling under the sun was involved, and I thought Sam would be the same.

Unfortunately, I struggled finding words to express my concern. "Just be careful. Okay?"

"I'm always careful. But seriously, Ev, you should be happy for me. For the first time in ages, I actually feel excited about something. I feel like I could go out into the world one day and find someone to love. Aren't you glad I won't spend the rest of my life alone?"

"That was never going to happen. You just think that way because of where we live, but go ten minutes on a bus and you're in gay mecca. You've just never ventured outside of this little bubble we live in, that's all."

"Ten minutes on a bus, eh? When we turn eighteen you have to promise to come to all the gay bars with me. *All* of them."

I chuckled. "'Course I will. Wouldn't want to miss out on all that dancing."

"Don't forget the chance to ogle gorgeous, sexually non-threatening men," Sam added with a wink as we entered the lunchroom.

Dylan, Amy, and Conor sat at a table, talking and eating. Sam and I approached, and I took the empty seat next to Dylan. I felt those hairs on the back of my neck tingling again and frowned. Just across the room, the boys Dylan had been suspended for fighting with eyed me in a way I found unsettling. Or maybe they were eyeing Dylan. Either way, it made me feel uncomfortable.

I tried to ignore them as I peeled open my sandwich. Conor shot me a sheepish glance and asked, "Did Yvonne say anything about Saturday?"

I bit my lip and took a bite. "She asked if you were okay after she left. She hoped she didn't hurt your feelings."

Conor dropped his face into his palms. "She pities me. I think that's even worse than if she was disgusted."

"Of course she wasn't disgusted. Don't be ridiculous. You just took her by surprise."

Conor's expression turned glum. "She doesn't think of me that way. I get it. I never would've done it if I wasn't drunk."

I sent him a commiserating look. "I know."

Conor glanced at Amy. "How long do you think it'll take for this embarrassment to fade?"

She pursed her lips. "Hmm, six to eight weeks, I reckon."

"Oh hell, kill me now."

"Don't be so melodramatic," Sam tutted. "I think it was very brave of you to make a move, even if it did end badly. At least now you know."

"Yeah," Conor sighed, dejected. "At least now I know."

"Your hair's different," Dylan commented, and I realised he'd been quietly studying me.

"Oh yeah, I just tied it up."

"What's this?" he asked, fingers sifting through the strands. "Is that chewing gum?"

"That cow Kirsty stuck it there," Sam told him, and I closed my eyes for a second. I didn't want any drama.

Dylan's gaze darkened as his attention came to me. "Kirsty did this?"

"She told me to stay away from you, but don't worry, she's just jealous—"

185

Before I had a chance to finish, Dylan was up from his seat. He pinpointed Kirsty on the other side of the room and made his way over. My throat constricted as I watched him confront her. None of us could hear what he said since he was too far away, but his body language was enough. He was reaming her out, and everyone who sat at the surrounding tables watched the drama unfold. Dylan made a furious hand gesture, and Kirsty's cheeks reddened. When he was done he marched back to our table, sat down and silently ate the rest of his lunch.

Nobody breathed a word. I wanted to ask what he said to her, but Dylan's entire being somehow commanded silence. I glanced across the room and sure enough, Kirsty was staring at us. Her expression was a mix of anger and mortification, but shame, too.

I had a feeling she wouldn't be sticking any more gum in my hair. And to some extent, that meant absolutely nothing. Dylan O'Dea had publicly defended *me*. Hating what had happened to me, he had launched to my defence. Up until that moment, I had only two people do that before in my life. Yvonne and Sam. My mam? She'd run, never looked back. But this beautiful boy—beautiful *man*—had stood up for me. There was no doubt in my mind.

I loved Dylan O'Dea. And probably would forever.

Thirteen

The week went by and Kirsty never enacted any revenge, so I hoped that was the end of it. Dylan came over every morning before school, but since Yvonne usually slept until around eleven, she had no clue of his comings and goings.

I felt a little guilty, but at the same time I loved it.

Going down on me seemed to be his new favourite thing. He was obsessed. I felt like I was someone else, some other more experienced, worldly teenager who had sex all the time. Like in American movies, where they all drive cars at sixteen and have active and varied love lives.

"Hi," I whispered as I answered the door to him on Friday morning. He gave me a sexy smile and moved to come inside when he spotted Yvonne. She was up early since she had a meeting at the bank. I suspected she was figuring out her options for taking out a loan, but I didn't want to think about it too much. Yvonne taking out a loan only meant one thing; she was considering moving to New York sooner than originally planned.

I think Conor's attempted kiss last week had a weird effect on her. We hadn't really discussed it, but I suspected it made her realise she needed to get moving, start working on her dreams or she'd never leave this place. She'd be stuck here forever, getting hit on by nineteen-year-olds and working every night until three in the morning.

In spite of my efforts not to think about it, I worried. If Yvonne left, I'd have to go live in a group home, or something of that variety, until I turned eighteen. It was only a couple of months, but still. What would I do when I did hit my next birthday? How would I support myself? Pay rent?

Of course, I could get a job, but I wasn't sure minimum wage would be enough.

"Morning, Dylan," Yvonne chirped knowingly. Maybe she wasn't so oblivious to his morning visits after all. Her expression was pleased, like she achieved her goal of surprising him.

"Hey, Yvonne. I just, uh, came to walk Ev to school."

She glanced at the clock. "A little early, isn't it?"

He cleared his throat. "I like to be punctual."

"Right, well, come in and have a cup of tea before you go. Ev hasn't had her breakfast yet."

He came inside and sat at the table, while I made tea and marmalade on toast. It was my favourite. Dylan kept shooting me meaningful looks, which I ignored. We were going to have to forego the sexy times this morning, and no amount of intense stares would change that. He hooked his foot around my ankle as I slid a small plate of toast to him. He ate it without protest, and washed it down with a gulp of tea.

"Well, we'd better get going," I said and went to give Yvonne a quick hug. "Good luck at the bank."

"Thanks, love," she smiled, and we went on our way.

"What's Yvonne going to the bank for?" Dylan asked once we got outside.

I shrugged and played it off like it was nothing. "Not sure. I think she might be trying for a loan."

"Like a mortgage?"

"No, more like a couple thousand so she can move. I don't think she wants to wait three years after all."

Dylan frowned as he walked. He was silent a long moment before he said, "But what will you do if she goes?"

"Get sent to a foster home? Pretty sure my mam won't volunteer to come back to Dublin and live with me until I turn eighteen."

"How can you sound so casual about it?" Worry etched his features.

"What else can I do? Yvonne's already taken care of me for three years. She's done her time."

"It's not a jail sentence, Ev."

"You know what I mean. I'd never dream of asking her to stay."

"You could always come with me," he suggested. "I'm sure there are ways for you to finish your last year of school online."

"And where would I get the money for that? I don't have a bunch of savings from my weekend job selling perfumes."

"I'll pay for you. We'll figure it out."

I stared at him and wondered if he was serious. He looked like he was. There wasn't a speck of uncertainty in his expression.

"I couldn't let you do that."

"Ev, I'm certain I can't do without you anyway. If you won't come, I may have to put you in my suitcase and take you against your will," he teased and poked me in the side.

I giggled. "Don't be ridiculous. You don't even know where you're going."

"But that's half the fun."

"What will you do? Go to the airport and buy a ticket on the next departing flight? That's the sort of schtick that gets you on a one-way journey to Lagos. Or better yet, Cork," I said with a shudder. I knew that for him, the only thing worse than going somewhere even more downtrodden than the Villas, was going to a city only one hundred and sixty miles away.

He wanted to travel far and wide, experience all the amazing things the world had to offer.

Dylan let out a soft breath and chilly air left his mouth. He rubbed his hands together as he replied, "I'll go wherever I can find the best opportunities."

I nodded and looked away, because the idea of losing both Dylan and Yvonne in the same year was heart-wrenching. Still, I sucked it up and put on a brave face. It wasn't like I could stop them from doing what they wanted. In fact, it'd be worse if I was the reason they didn't.

We made our way down to Sam's flat, but when I knocked, his mam said he'd already left. I thought nothing of it, because sometimes he had early choir practices. For someone so tiny, he had a set of lungs on him. I was the only one who knew he secretly dreamed of singing as a profession, but going to stage school was expensive. I was pretty sure when his mam encouraged him to go to college, she didn't have performing arts in mind.

Dylan and I walked to school hand in hand. When we arrived, I frowned, because Sam climbed out from the behind the bushes close to the front gates. Shane emerged soon after, but both of them walked inside like they didn't even know each other.

"Did I just see what I think I did?"

"They're having a secret affair," I sighed. "Sam's in love with the idea. There's no talking to him."

"You know if it ever gets out, Shane will likely beat Sam up just to show how 'not gay' he is."

So, Dylan could see how reckless Sam was being, too. I was glad it wasn't just me, but at the same time it made me worry even more.

"Sam says he's not emotionally invested, but I'm not so sure. I mean, he's the very definition of emotional investment. He can't pick his favourite sandwich without feeling torn between two lovers."

Dylan's expression was curious. "I wouldn't have thought that."

"That's because he puts on a good front, but believe me, underneath it all he's soft as candy floss."

We reached our lockers, and I opened mine, noticing Kirsty at hers. She cast me a quick look then proceeded to ignore us. Dylan appeared thoughtful for a minute then said, "What if we distract him somehow? I usually go running in Phoenix Park most Sunday mornings. I could invite him to join me. Maybe it would be good for him to have a male friend he can talk to about stuff."

"I didn't know you ran," I commented.

He shrugged. "It's basically the only exercise I do."

"Well, it works," I muttered, and he grinned. "Also, that's a very kind offer. I'll ask Sam if he's interested."

"Good. Let me know what he says."

Kirsty slammed her locker shut and sauntered off. Hmmm, I still sensed a hint of an attitude from her, then again, that was sort of her personality. Dylan and I went to our morning classes, but all the while my mind stayed on Sam. Maybe I was being overly protective. Maybe everything would be fine and this thing with Shane would fizzle out on its own.

After school, I went to visit Gran. I had a box of toffees and a new crossword puzzle book to give her. When I got there, she was sitting by the window in the common area reading a book.

"Hi, Gran," I said as I approached to give her a hug. Her face lit up in a smile when she saw me. I wished my hugs could bring back the vibrant, strong woman she'd been when I was little. I missed her.

"Evelyn, you're a sight for sore eyes," she greeted, hugging me back before I went to take the seat opposite her.

"It's so quiet in here," I commented, and she chuckled.

"You should come at night. The place transforms. It's like a Roman orgy after hours."

"Gran!"

"It's true. All these old timers are mad for it. They don't have to worry about getting pregnant."

I laughed some more, delighted she was in a good mood. Her speech was perfect today and she looked well rested. It was a stark contrast to other days, when she was in pain and could hardly get her words out.

"I brought some things," I said, pulling the toffees and crossword puzzles from my school bag.

"You're too good to me."

"I wanted to bring you some flowers, but I've been so busy I've hardly had time to garden."

Her eyes got a twinkle. "Yvonne says you've got a new boyfriend."

I nodded shyly. "Yes, Dylan. Remember the boy who came to visit with me?"

"Yes. A very polite young man."

I frowned. "Some girls at school aren't happy about me being with him."

"Well, of course they aren't. He's quite the looker."

"I'm worried it's bringing me the wrong kind of attention."

"Ignore them. You concentrate on your studies and don't let the bullies have their way. When you acknowledge them, you give them power."

"I wish it was as easy as that," I sighed.

"It's not easy, but I know you can do it. You're a strong girl, so much like my Yvonne."

"Why do you think I'm not like Mam?" I asked quietly.

"Oh, Ev. Who's to tell? We are who we are for a variety of reasons. It isn't down to any one thing."

"I think I'm in love with Dylan," I blurted then and her expression softened.

"And why do you sound so sad about it?"

"Because he's leaving when he finishes school. He's like Yvonne, too. He thinks there's a better life somewhere far from here."

"Well, they have to find out for themselves whether it's true. You can travel to the ends of the earth, but you'll still be you." She tapped the side of my head. "You have to face the challenges in here before you'll find happiness out there," she went on, gesturing around herself.

"How are you so wise?"

"Pain has a way of making you see things clearly."

My brow furrowed. I hated the idea of her being in pain, but I knew it was a daily reality for her.

"Let's open that packet of toffees, eh?" I said, not wanting to think about it anymore.

***

A month passed and Dylan and I fell into a blissful routine. Sex was our new obsession. Even at school he could hardly keep his hands off me. After the third or fourth time, it stopped hurting and started to feel good. Too good, almost. Each day I fell deeper and deeper in love with him. I didn't think there was a single part of my heart he hadn't yet claimed.

Sam and Shane's affair was still ongoing, and still a secret. I often caught him smiling to himself, and I knew he was thinking about it. Sometimes we talked about it, and I tried not to judge. I had to accept that Sam was old enough to make his own decisions.

Anyway, in a year's time he'd likely go to college. He'd meet some pretty, caring, sensitive boy, they'd fall hopelessly in love and he'd forget all about Shane. That was my vision for him.

I was on my way to lunch one day when someone grabbed me by the hand and pulled me into the chemistry lab. I turned and saw Dylan, and my heart skipped a beat. He stared at me lovingly.

"I've got a surprise for you," he said and guided me to a lab table. No teachers were around, and it felt weird for it to be just the two of us.

"Oh." I couldn't imagine what sort of surprise had to be given in a chemistry lab. There was a whole mess of items on the table, and I recognised some flowers from my allotment.

"I wondered where those had gone. Thought I had a flower thief on my hands."

He gave an apologetic smile. "You did. It was me, but I promise it was for a good cause."

"What is all this?"

"I'm creating my own perfume," he replied, and my gaze widened. That wasn't what I expected at all.

"Really? Wow. That's . . . wow."

"Don't sound so apprehensive. I promise it's not awful."

I shook my head at him. "Well, of course it isn't, but I mean, isn't making perfume really complicated?"

I got that he sold them for his job, and he had a good nose for it, but it just surprised me that he would make his own. When we were little, Sam and I sometimes stole rose petals from Gran and put them in jars to make perfume, but it never really worked.

"It is, but I got to thinking about what you said, about me inventing my own product. I know everything there is to know about perfume, and chemistry is my best subject, so I thought, why don't I just make my own? I also needed a topic for my end-of-term project, so this was perfect."

I never thought about perfume in terms of chemistry, but that was where it all started. In a lab. Maybe Dylan's project wasn't so unusual after all. Maybe he could make something of this, use his innate skills for something amazing.

"Can I smell it?" I was completely charmed by his excited energy. His hair was askew, his uniform rumpled. He looked like he'd been up all night working.

Dylan presented me with a small glass jar. It had a pale liquid inside, but the cap was screwed tight. I glanced at the concoction of jasmine, echinacea, and wildflowers on the table, and smiled at the thought of him sneaking up to the roof to steal them from my allotment. I picked up a bottle and read the label aloud. "Angelica root essential oil. What do you use this for?"

"That's for the musk base note. The perfume is an oriental, like the one I bought for you."

"Oh," I said and smiled. I'd never heard of oriental perfume until I met Dylan, but I now knew it was my favourite. I studied the flowers again. "Is that my anise hyssop?"

Dylan nodded. "Yeah, sorry, I just needed a small piece."

"What for? It smells like liquorice." *Not very perfume-y*, I thought.

He scratched his head, his eyes alight as he answered, "I'm finding that a tiny bit of something that doesn't fit, something odd, or maybe even slightly disgusting, can actually bring out the scent more. I mean, sure, all the ingredients smell fine, but if you can find that one drop of something unusual that raises them from ordinary to extraordinary, that's when the magic happens."

"So, something savoury to bring out the sweet?" I asked. "Like a pinch of salt in a recipe for cake?"

"Exactly," Dylan enthused. "And it works the opposite way, too. For instance, you might put a spoonful of sugar in a bread recipe, but it doesn't come out sweet, it simply helps you taste more of the savoury."

A warmth spread through my chest from his enthusiasm. I picked up the perfume.

"Okay, let's give this thing a whirl."

Dylan seemed uncharacteristically nervous as I screwed open the jar. In the last month, I had learned a lot about him. He was loyal, altruistic, plus confident with a dose of humility at the same time. He was a man I never wanted to lose. But watching him now, his delight in creating something that would no doubt be wonderful, was a little daunting. He was destined for significant things. Extraordinary things. He would outgrow St Mary's, and I feared mostly he'd outgrow me, too. But in this moment, sensing his nerves, I knew for now, my opinion mattered, and I felt special because of it.

Lifting the jar to my nose, I inhaled deeply and was instantly swept away on a cloud of a beautiful scent. It was subtle but powerful, each ingredient having its moment to shine. At first you were met with jasmine, then delicate, sweet echinacea, and underneath there was a faint but generous hint of musk.

"Wow," I breathed, eyes rising to meet Dylan's.

He bit his lip, his expression unsure. "What do you think?"

"It's beautiful. Exquisite. I love it."

"You're lying."

"I'm not. You've seriously outdone yourself. I love it more than the one I have at home that cost ninety euros to buy. I genuinely think you've got something special here, Dylan."

He came and cupped my face in his hands. "Thank you," he whispered. "I keep wondering if Mam would like it if she was still alive. Then I remember she couldn't smell and smack myself for forgetting."

My face turned sympathetic. "Even so, I'm sure she would've enjoyed you describing it to her."

His face softened. "She did love that."

"You miss her a lot, don't you?" His pain was so clearly etched into his frown. Most of the time he did a good job of hiding it, but right now he was vulnerable. I could see every ounce of his torment.

"All the time. I wish she was still here, but at least she's not in pain anymore. Seeing her suffer was the worst part. Towards the end . . . it was awful. I wouldn't wish watching a loved one pass away on my worst enemy."

I swallowed; emotion clutched me as I spoke. "Sometimes, when Gran's having a bad day, I just think, why can't I take half the pain so we could share it? Then it wouldn't be so bad. You feel helpless when there's nothing you can do to make it stop."

Dylan nodded. "If I could've swapped places with her, I would have. I'd take all her tumours so she could live."

"She wouldn't have wanted that. No mother should have to lose a child."

"No child should have to lose a mother," he countered sadly and dropped his forehead to mine. I could smell his minty breath, and I loved his skin against my skin.

"That's not how the world works."

"Sometimes I hate the world."

"The world is easy to hate, especially when you think about all the pain in it. But there's a lot to be thankful for, so I choose to think about that instead. You should, too."

His hand drifted into my hair, his expression fierce as he whispered, "I'm thankful for you, Ev. I love you so much."

My breath caught, and then he kissed me. He backed me up against the wall beside his lab table and laid siege to my mouth. I pressed my palms to the cold, magnolia wall and wondered how I got here. Dylan was sensitive and creative and intelligent, and he loved *me*. Not any of the other girls at school. *Me*.

I wasn't sure what I did to deserve him, but I wasn't going to protest. Not when his hands groped my body, grasping at my dips and lines, feeling for places to stay awhile.

He broke the kiss, breathless, and took my hand in his. "Come with me."

I followed as he led me to the back of the classroom, through a door and into the storage closet. There was a table on one side, and on the other a wall lined with shelves containing all manner of chemical substances. I wasn't so sure it was safe to be in here.

"Shouldn't this room be locked?"

"Mr Tully trusts me."

"Well, he shouldn't."

Dylan smirked. "You think I'd burn the school down or something?"

"No, but everyone makes mistakes."

"Just shut up and kiss me, Evelyn," he said and without preamble lifted me up onto the table. He pressed his mouth to mine. I felt his hunger as he fumbled open my waistband and slipped his hand inside. Gasping into his kiss, I slid my tongue along his and opened my legs wider. I wanted him to touch me.

"More," I whispered, and his fingers moved past the seam of my underwear. He rubbed my clit and I heaved a moan. "Yes, like that."

I closed my eyes and got lost in him. He pushed his fingers inside me and I gasped. We should both be at lunch but here we were here, on the verge of having sex in a chemical-filled storage closet.

"Ev," he rasped.

"Hmm?"

"Undo my pants."

My stomach flipped and I nervously reached out. My fingers fiddled with his fly until I got it free, then I ran them over the trail of hair at his stomach. He shuddered at my touch and I hesitated.

"Don't stop," he whispered and I pressed my palm flat to his belly. That alone caused his breath to come out in a rush. I kept my eyes closed and reached for him. He swore when I wrapped my fingers around his cock.

"You don't need to be gentle, Ev," he murmured huskily and dropped his mouth to my neck. Tingles skittered down my spine and I slowly moved my hand up and down. Dylan groaned and pulled a condom from his pocket, but I paused to stop him. Biting my lip, I met his eyes.

"We don't need that," I whispered.

Over the last month, we'd gone through our fair share of condoms. I hadn't told him yet, but I went back to the GP clinic and got on the pill. I knew it didn't mean we could go around having unprotected sex all the time, but I wanted to know what it felt like now that the pain of losing my virginity was long gone.

Dylan's brows furrowed. "Ev, of course we—"

"I'm on the pill."

His brows furrowed even more. "You are? Since when?"

"Just over a week. I went to see the doctor. I thought it would be a good idea since we're . . . you know, doing this so much."

I couldn't believe I got embarrassed saying it, especially considering our current position. Dylan was still studying me when I asked, "Are you angry?"

"Of course not. I just wish you'd told me. I could've gone with you and . . ."

I placed a finger to his lips to shush him. "Stop fretting. It's done now. Also, lunch is almost over." I gave him a cheeky grin. He shook his head and grinned, too, then started kissing me again. He palmed my thighs, his movements even more eager than they'd been before.

I gasped when he mouthed my neck and slid inside of me with a guttural groan.

I loved being with him. My only concern was getting caught, but that wasn't likely to happen during lunch. Once the clock struck twelve thirty, most teachers fled like bats out of hell, eager for an hour's respite from dealing with teenagers all day.

I buried my face in his shoulder, biting down a little when he moved his hips. His pace quickened, and I moaned at how good it felt. He reached down to rub my clit, and I lost my mind. My body tensed and Dylan swore.

"Jesus."

"I think I'm gonna come," I whispered.

"Yes," he groaned. "Come on me."

That did it. The way he spoke was an aphrodisiac. I shook as I orgasmed on his fingers. He bent his mouth to my neck and gave a gentle bite. I whimpered and clutched him tighter.

Moments later he came, too. He wrapped his arms around me as he filled me up, then fell against me with a quiet shudder.

With his arms surrounding me, and his entire body against mine, I felt overwhelmed. "I love you," I blurted. He made a happy hum in the back of his throat. His face was pressed against the side of mine, and I felt his muscles move as he smiled.

"I love you, too, Ev. Always will."

A few minutes of quiet passed as we just held each other, and then Dylan helped me right my clothes. When we were both presentable, we walked back into the classroom hand in hand. It was thankfully empty.

Like usual, I was swept up in daydreams of Dylan for the rest of my evening. If my grades went down, I knew who to blame. All the lessons blended into meaningless babble when I had Dylan in my head, telling me to touch him, urging me to come.

It was a miracle I managed to get through my classes at all. And then, when it came time for my final class of the day, Biology, I sat at my usual table and noticed the teacher hadn't arrived yet. A few minutes passed, and the other students became rowdy, excited that we'd all somehow been forgotten about.

The door opened and the rowdiness faded. However, it was wasn't the teacher who walked in, but Dylan. A flush instantly claimed my cheeks when our eyes briefly met, memories of what we did during lunch flooding my head. Dylan turned and addressed the room.

"Mr. Gleeson had to go home sick, so I've been asked to supervise until the end of class. You can take out your books and do homework."

"Piss off. I'm not listening to you. You're not even a teacher," said Jackson Keegan, one of the boys Dylan had been suspended for fighting with over a month ago. They hadn't gotten into any more scrapes, but he was constantly eyeballing Dylan when he passed us by in the corridors. Dylan always ignored him, which was probably why they hadn't fought again. I knew Jackson was just biding his time, waiting for his chance to start something.

"Yeah, piss off," another boy added.

Dylan looked at him in a disinterested way that somehow commanded respect. "I could give a shit. I'm just telling you what I was told to tell you. Do what you want."

Jackson scowled, irritated that Dylan wasn't giving him a reason to fight. I squirmed in my seat, feeling edgy. We had another thirty minutes left of class, and I knew Jackson was going to use every opportunity to rile Dylan.

Dylan sat down at the teacher's desk, opened one of his own books and proceeded to ignore everyone. He didn't make eye contact with me again, but I couldn't help noticing how sexy he looked from this angle. Maybe it was because he was at the teacher's desk. It sort of made my mind wander to interesting places.

And I wondered why he'd been asked to supervise. Then again, he'd probably just been walking by the principal's office at the exact time someone was needed and the receptionist simply grabbed him.

Everyone was still making a lot of noise, which prompted the teacher from the room across the hall, Mrs Green, to stride in. "Okay, quiet down you lot. I'm leaving my door open, so I don't want to hear anything above a whisper." She eyed a few of the troublesome students to hammer home her point then turned to Dylan. "If anyone acts out, just come and get me."

Everyone was mostly quiet after that. Mrs Green was known for giving not just one evening, but an entire week's worth of detention as punishment for bad behaviour. Dylan's attention returned to his text book, and I watched him a minute.

Man, he was handsome.

His gaze flicked up, and he caught me looking. I saw him smirk before I rolled my eyes in an effort to cover up the fact I was flushing like an idiot. How could I have been with him an entire month and still feel bashful for checking him out?

My thoughts stopped short when Dylan's expression hardened, and there was a sneering laugh from Jackson. "I forgot your little girlfriend was in this class. She's so quiet, you never notice her. What's your name again, babe?"

I made eye contact with Dylan and ignored Jackson, but my posture was stiff. I hated this, hated the tension. And I could see Dylan's temper rising just from the fact that Jackson mentioned me.

"She's got a great arse, doesn't she?" Jackson went on, addressing Dylan. "Like a ripe peach."

A few of the boys in class chuckled, while Dylan's face hardened further. I eyed him intently, trying to communicate with him to ignore whatever Jackson said.

I knew it was useless when he sneered, "Let me know when you're done with her, yeah? I wouldn't mind a go."

Dylan carefully closed over his textbook and rose from his seat. His measured movements were in contrast with how quickly he advanced on Jackson. I barely had a chance to blink before he gripped him by the shirt collar, lifted him from his seat and slammed him back against the classroom wall.

"You ever talk about her again and I'll fucking end you," he fumed. "Do you hear me?"

My heart beat frantically in my chest. I prayed for Mrs. Green to hear the commotion and come in as I rose from my seat and pleaded with Dylan, "He's not worth it. Just ignore him."

His blink was the only indication that he'd heard me, but he didn't loosen his hold. Instead he slammed Jackson into the wall a second time. "Do you fucking hear me?" he grunted.

Jackson chocked, his face red, as he coughed and laughed cruelly. "You're gonna regret this, O'Dea."

The sound of heels clipping on the linoleum sounded as Mrs. Green approached the room. Quick as a flash, Dylan let go of Jackson and returned to his seat. Jackson sat, too, and when she entered everyone acted like nothing had happened.

"Everything okay in here?" Mrs Green asked, and nobody made a peep. She glanced at Dylan. "Are they all behaving?"

He nodded, but I recognised the strain on his face. "Yep."

She studied him a moment, then glanced around the room. Her suspicion was clear, but she didn't have proof that anything happened. "Next time I hear a single sound out of you lot the entire class is getting a week of detention," she announced then strode from the room.

We were all quiet after that. I managed to catch Dylan's eye after she left, and he looked tired. I hated I was his weak link, the thing Jackson decided to attack. I was the one person at school Dylan was liable to lose his shit over if anyone so much as looked at me the wrong way. Now Jackson had something to get Dylan back for, and it had me all twisted up inside.

I held his gaze and he held mine, a silent conversation between us.

You shouldn't have done that, I said.

But I had to, he replied.

The bell rang and Jackson eyeballed Dylan all the way out the door. I waited until everyone had left to approach him. I slid my fingers through his and gave his hand a soft squeeze.

"When are you ever going to learn that violence isn't the answer?"

Dylan ran a hand through his hair. "I know it isn't, Ev, but it's all people like Jackson understand."

For a long while after, his words echoed in my head. I couldn't decide if he was right. It did seem that people like Jackson wouldn't listen to reason, they only wanted to fight. He and his gang had set their sights on Dylan a long time ago. They pinpointed him as easy prey, because even though he was big and strong, he didn't have twenty other people to back him up. These types, they always ran in groups. Individually they were cowards, but there was strength in numbers.

I just hoped Dylan could keep his head down long enough to escape their grasp.

Fourteen

Still feeling unsettled when we got home that evening, I kissed Dylan goodbye at his flat and headed upstairs. Things only got worse when I walked into the kitchen and found Yvonne at the table doing budgets.

There weren't many banks in our area, but Yvonne being Yvonne, had been to each one looking for the lowest interest, the best repayment structure and other financial necessities I had no idea about. I hadn't said anything to her about my future, as there was no way I would voice my concerns. Not now. Not after so many interviews. But today she looked more excited than before, and my stomach twisted uncomfortably. I knew it was selfish, but I secretly wished for bad news.

I wasn't ready to lose her. I wasn't sure I ever would be.

"How did the meeting go today at the bank? This was the one with the lowest interest rates, right?"

"Yes. And it went great! I was approved for my loan." She was smiling, and I hated myself a little that I wanted her to be looking a little more like I felt. *Dismal.*

As soon as she said it, there it was. Pain. Yvonne got her loan. What if she left before the school year was through?

I didn't say anything as I took off my coat and set my bag down by the couch.

"There's some chicken and rice on the stove," she went on.

"I'm not really hungry," I replied. Subdued, I went into my bedroom. I lay down on my bed and pressed my face into the pillow, a million thoughts racing through my mind. I picked up my phone, and for the first time in a long time, I felt like contacting Mam.

I didn't know why.

Maybe I was just feeling sorry for myself.

I pulled her number and rubbed my finger over the call button. My throat tightened as I experimentally pressed 'call'. It rang just once before I came to my senses and hit 'end'. I threw my phone into the drawer on my bedside table and closed my eyes. A few minutes later my bedroom door opened. Yvonne stepped inside, her face a picture of concern.

"You feeling under the weather, Ev?"

I opened my eyes and shook my head. "Just tired."

She came and sat next to me on the bed. Reaching out, she tucked some hair behind my ear. "You seem out of sorts."

I bit my lip, feeling like a baby. I just wanted to cry and beg her not to go. I might look grown up, nearly an adult, but deep down I was still a little girl who needed her mammy. And Yvonne was the closest thing I had to a mother these days.

Tears sprang in my eyes, and I tried to push them back. It was no use. Yvonne saw them right away.

"Oh, Ev, what's wrong?"

"Are you leaving?" I whispered past the tears.

She frowned in confusion. "What are you talking about?"

"The loan. You got approved, so you must be planning to go to New York soon."

She stared at me for a second as understanding dawned, then vehemently shook her head. "Honey, no, the loan isn't for New York. That's what my savings are for. The loan is so I can buy us a second-hand car. I thought it'd be nice if we could take Mam out on day trips once a week. Plus, it'd be good to be able to drive to and from work without having to use the buses. I didn't say anything because I wanted it to be a surprise."

Embarrassment swallowed me whole. I felt so silly for jumping to conclusions. Yvonne studied me, her face sad. "I'd never plan to leave without telling you, Ev. You know I wouldn't. The three-year plan is still in place. And I'll make sure you're well set up in your life before I go anywhere. If you aren't, I'm liable to take you with me."

I gave a watery laugh that was full of relief and she pulled me into her arms. "Love you," she whispered and pressed a kiss to my temple. "I'm not going to abandon you. Never, Ev. You hear me? You're the best thing in my life, and my home will always be your home whenever you need it."

I knew at that moment, that it wasn't my mam I'd wanted to talk to a few moments ago. It was reassurance I needed. Hope. *Home.* And that home was Yvonne. I knew she wasn't lying. I knew she'd never abandon me."

I hugged her tight just as the doorbell rang. She wiped my tears away and got up to see who it was. A minute later Sam came into my room and flopped onto my bed. Yvonne returned and sat next to him.

"You been crying, Ev?" he asked, brow furrowed. I wasn't the sort to have emotional outbursts. In fact, I rarely cried. I didn't often have occasion for it.

"I took out a loan to buy a car, but Ev thought I wanted the money so I could move to New York early. It was a whole big mix-up," Yvonne explained.

Sam poked me in the shoulder. "You silly billy. That's not Vonny's style."

"That's what I said," Yvonne added and I thought she looked a little emotional herself. I knew she was feeling guilty that she hadn't told me about the car.

"I shouldn't have jumped to conclusions," I sniffed.

"It's not your fault. Now that I think about it, your conclusion was the obvious one," Yvonne replied and pulled me in for another hug. Sam joined in, because that was who he was, and we sat like that for a minute together.

"Well, do you know what I think? I think we should order Dominoes. Pizza makes everyone feel better," Sam suggested cheekily.

"Hey! Stop exploiting the situation for your appetite's gain," I said with a chuckle.

Sam grinned. "What can I say? I'm a pizza opportunist."

Yvonne laughed and dabbed at her eyes. "Dominoes actually sounds really good right now."

Sam rubbed his hands together in glee. "Yes, and we can catch up on what those housewives on Wisteria Lane have been up to this week."

How long had it been since we'd had a night with the three of us eating junk and binge-watching our favourite show? This was us. This was what we needed tonight.

"Sounds like a plan," I said.

"Where would I be without you two, eh?" Yvonne asked fondly.

"A very horrible place. Best not to think of it," Sam teased and pulled out his phone to order the food.

Fifteen

"Are we still on for our morning run tomorrow?" Sam asked, leaning against the locker next to Dylan's.

"Yeah, but I've got to drop into work first, so I'll meet you at the entrance to Phoenix Park around ten," Dylan replied as he pulled several books out of his bag.

I tried to feel happy that their runs had become a weekly event, but I was a little distracted by Kirsty and her friends. Like usual, they stood just a few lockers down, whispering to each other and snickering, obviously being mean about me. It was a regular occurrence that I tried to ignore, but ever since Dylan's public rejection of her, she was constantly shooting me dirty looks and slagging me off to people. It wasn't so bad when compared with the sheer hatred she aimed at Dylan, but still. The girl could hold a serious grudge. I mean, even after all these weeks she was still feeling sore.

I frowned, distracted, as a lump formed in my throat. I felt like saying something to her. I just hated tension and her animosity was so pointless. It wasn't going to achieve anything. Before I could summon up the courage, she and her friends walked away. I slumped back against the wall and let out a frustrated sigh.

"What's wrong?" Dylan asked, sensing my agitation.

He came and placed a reassuring hand on my shoulder, but I shook myself out of it. "Nothing. Let's get to class."

Later that day, on my way to Biology, I crossed paths with Kirsty again. Well, not so much crossed paths. More like I walked by her, and she didn't notice me. It wasn't the time to approach and have a word though, because she was snuggling up to Jackson Keegan. Was he her boyfriend now? Ugh.

She whispered something in his ear and he nodded, listening intently. I tried not to be too worried about such a vile pairing, because those two were so awful they probably deserved each other. Or maybe their shared awfulness would cancel itself out.

Yeah, probably not.

***

"You're really pulling out all the stops," Amy commented as I put together a picnic for Dylan and me. I had cheese and grapes and tiny sandwiches. I even bought a bottle of cheap Prosecco at the off-licence without getting asked for ID. Happy days.

"Dylan's been studying so hard. He deserves a treat," I replied. I'd decided to surprise him with a picnic date, and it wasn't even his birthday. Yep, I was the perfect girlfriend. He was staying late after school for a study session, so I'd gone home to make a head start on my surprise.

"If you ask me, he'll be happy with a cheeseburger and a handy J," Amy said and I chuckled.

"Classy. Now why didn't I think of that?"

215

Over the last few weeks, Amy and I had become friends. Not best friends, mind, but friends nonetheless. She liked to pop over and comment sarcastically on whatever I was doing. It was our thing.

"Because you lack creativity, obviously," she replied, teasing me.

"How has everything been going with Eddie, by the way?" I asked.

After our conversation at Conor's birthday, I'd turned my hand to matchmaking and set Amy up with a boy she fancied from school. They'd gone out a few times, so I wondered if it was getting serious. The romantic in me enjoyed the idea of being the one who brought them together.

"It's going fine. We've had a few snogs, but I've decided to keep it casual. I'm not looking for a boyfriend. I mean, I'll be leaving in the summer anyway."

My chest deflated in disappointment, both because she was keeping it casual with Eddie and because she was leaving the Villas. When the school year ended, Amy was moving to Wexford to work for her uncle's company, which sold farming equipment. I couldn't exactly see her being a good sales rep, but she seemed excited for the job. Or maybe she was just excited to have a regular wage. Either way, I was going to miss her, especially given we'd only just gotten to know each other.

"I'm going to miss you when you leave this summer."

She rolled her eyes. "Piss off."

I set down the napkins I was folding. "No, really. I am. You have to let me visit."

"Sure. If you don't mind my Steve Buscemi-looking cousins coming onto you. My aunt had five boys. She was so desperate for a girl that she kept trying, but every time out popped another tiny penis."

I chuckled and grimaced. "Nice."

"You know I don't censor."

"Yes, and it's why I love you. Come here."

"No. You've got an amorous look in your eye. I don't like it."

"I want to give you a hug."

"Hard pass."

Before she could protest further, I came at her and threw my hands around her shoulders. She went quiet, but she let me hug her. I knew she liked the affection, she just wouldn't admit it.

There was a knock at the door, and I let go of Amy to answer it. I flung it open and practically jumped on Dylan when I saw him. He chuckled as he held me in his grip.

"Now, there's a warm welcome," he murmured and dipped to give me a kiss.

"How did you do on your chemistry project?"

A grin spread across his face. "Aced it."

I smiled. "I knew you would."

I pressed my mouth to his neck, and he made a low rumble. "Why don't we go into your bedroom?" he whispered just as Amy popped her head around the corner.

"Oh, knock yourselves out. I'm leaving anyway. Well done on your project and all that."

She slipped by us and out the door. Dylan returned his gaze to me and waggled his brows. "Well, now that we're all alone . . ."

I poked him in the chest. "No bedroom shenanigans. I have a surprise planned, but first, you need to go home and shower. You've been sitting in a stuffy classroom all day and you stink."

"Hey," he protested, but he was still smiling.

"You know I'm right. Now go on, shower and meet me on the roof in thirty minutes."

His grin was devilish. "Is that where I'm getting my surprise?"

"It might be."

"Okay, but it better be good." He winked and I swiped him on the arse as he left. He chuckled all the way out the door. I loved when he was like this, cheerful and flirtatious. I was seeing less and less of the cynical, moody Dylan, and I liked to think our relationship made him feel like life wasn't so bad.

There was something that felt so natural and pure about being with him. When we were together, all our troubles seemed less consuming. It really was like having a soulmate, and there was this constant light and airy feeling inside me now.

The only thing that tainted it was the thought of him leaving. But maybe he wouldn't. Maybe he'd come to realise that forging a life here in Dublin wasn't such an awful prospect . . . maybe.

I shook myself from my thoughts and changed into my best sundress and a cardigan. Gathering everything I'd prepared for the picnic, I headed to the roof to set up before Dylan got there. I spread the blanket on the concrete, then placed a small arrangement of flowers in the middle. When I was done, I stood back to admire my handiwork.

"You made us a picnic?" came Dylan's voice from behind. I turned and shot him a smile. He'd changed out of his uniform and into some jeans and a T-shirt, his hair still damp from the shower.

He was so beautiful.

I knew it wasn't exactly the right word to describe a boy, but he was beautiful to me. I loved everything about his face, from the slightly crooked line of his nose, to the indent between his eyebrows, to his masculine-shaped lips.

"Yep. Do you like it?"

"Of course, I do," he replied and sat. He tugged me onto his lap and plucked a grape from the container. He brought it to my mouth, and I ate it happily.

"I can't wait to spend this summer with you," he said and my heart skipped a beat. Did that mean he wasn't leaving?

I looked away and bit my lip as I asked quietly, "You're staying?"

He caught my chin between his thumb and forefinger and brought my eyes back to his. "I can't leave. Not without you."

"What will you do?"

"I'll go full-time at work, keep saving until you finish school. Then we can leave together."

"But Dylan, I told you I can't. I have Gran to care for and—"

"Hush," he said and pressed a finger to my lips. "Let's not worry about all that right now. You've made an amazing picnic and the weather is good for once. For tonight, let's just enjoy living in the moment."

Hmm, I did like the sound of that. Sometimes it was exhausting when your brain wouldn't stop churning over. We ate and chatted about what we might do when school broke for the summer. It was still months away, but it was nice to make plans.

Dylan pulled me to lie down, and I cuddled into his side as we stared at the sky. It was getting dark, but there weren't any stars yet.

"I got a missed call from my mam a few days ago," I said, my voice quiet.

Dylan stroked my arm peacefully when his movements stilled. "Why didn't you tell me?"

I lifted a shoulder. "I don't know. I just didn't really know what to think. I can't imagine why she'd call."

"Maybe she wants to visit."

"When she wants to visit she doesn't call, she just turns up," I said and fell silent. We didn't speak for a moment. "I called her the other week, but hung up before she could answer. I was upset with Yvonne and I . . . I don't know. I guess I was just feeling sorry for myself."

Dylan's stroking started again. "Do you want to see her?"

I shook my head. "Not really. She's not a very nice person."

"If my mam were still alive, I'd want to see her, even if she wasn't a nice person."

"But your mam was nice. You don't know what it's like when they just leave. Yvonne's love was the only thing that stitched me back together. When Mam left, when I realised that she'd been wanting to leave for so long, my heart broke."

"You can't forgive her," Dylan said, like he understood.

"No," I whispered. "I don't think I can."

"Then it's simple, don't answer her calls."

"What if she shows up though?"

"Then you can come stay with me until she leaves again."

I smiled. "Not sure your dad would agree to that."

"My dad loves you. He wouldn't mind."

I arched a brow. "He wouldn't love the idea of me sleeping in your bed and that's a fact."

Dylan traced the line of my jaw with his finger. "Hmm, you're probably right. I can't wait until we have our own place and can sleep together every night."

I grinned. "Oh really? Tell me more."

"There'll be a strict no-pyjama policy. Also, oral sex every night. For both of us."

"Well, how can I argue with that?"

He bent to give me a kiss and whispered. "You can't."

The kiss deepened, and before I knew it I was squirming beneath him, wishing we were somewhere more private. Dylan's phone buzzed, distracting us. I broke away and caught my breath as I told him to check who it was. He opened the message and grinned.

"What is it?" I asked and peeked over his shoulder. He hid the screen from my view.

"Don't think I'm supposed to show you."

"Oh, come on, now you have to," I said and reached for the phone.

He held it in the air, so I couldn't get to it. I struggled again, but he only held it higher.

"Now, now, don't be nosy," Dylan chided as I stretched across his body, reaching for the phone but finding no purchase. His hard chest beneath me was a little distracting, but I was determined to find out what the text said.

"Fine," I huffed, giving up. "You keep your secrets. See if I care."

Dylan let out a sigh. "Okay, I'll show you. But only because you've told me before that you don't like big surprises."

I narrowed my gaze curiously as I took the offered phone. It was a group text from Sam.

OKAY, LISTEN UP, PEEPS. It's our girl Evelyn's B-day in two weeks and I'm planning a big old-fashioned knees up. Yvonne's keeping her out of the flat all day so that we can decorate, and I'll need all your help. Be there at 12pm sharp or consider yourself blacklisted by yours truly. Sam. Xoxo.

"Oh, that sneaky little . . ."

"He just wants to do something nice for you," Dylan said. "Why didn't you say your birthday was coming up?"

I blew out a breath. "I honestly didn't even think of it."

Dylan rubbed his chin ponderously, a twinkle in his eye. "Now I've got to think of something special to do for you."

"You don't need to do anything, just be you. That's special enough for me."

He grinned and pulled my mouth in for a soft kiss. "God, we make me sick sometimes."

I chuckled. "We make me sick sometimes, too."

Sixteen

"Well, what do you think?" Yvonne asked with a smile as she stuck her head out of her brand-new car and honked the horn. Well, it wasn't *brand* new. It was a second-hand Volkswagen but in pretty good nick. She collected it from the lot this morning, and I'd come down to the front of the flats to check it out.

"Pretty snazzy," I said and grinned.

"Come on, jump in and we'll go for a drive."

I opened the passenger side door without hesitation and slid into the seat before securing my seatbelt. It was a mild morning, tendrils of pretty sunlight streaming through the windows as we left the flats behind us.

"This is so great. We should go on a road trip down the country some weekend."

"Sounds like a plan," she agreed just as my phone rang. It was Dylan. I hit 'answer' and held it up to my ear, thinking he and Sam had probably just finished their run in the park.

"Dylan! You'll never guess what me and Yvonne are—"

"Ev," he choked. "Come quickly . . . I think Sam's—"

"What's wrong?" My stomach tightened instantly at the pained rasp in his voice.

"I've called an ambulance, but they haven't arrived yet. Jesus Christ, I can't feel his pulse, I can't feel his pulse," Dylan rambled chaotically, and I felt like I was being submerged under water. His words spread terror right through my body.

Then, something inside of me swallowed up all the panic and jumped into action. "Where are you?" I had no idea what was going on or what had happened. All I knew was I had to get to him as quickly as possible.

"We're j-just in front of the Wellington Monument. Please h-hurry."

Yvonne glanced from me to the road in concern. "What's wrong, Ev?"

To Dylan, I said, "We'll be there in five minutes," and then I told Yvonne where to go. She drove like a pro, avoiding all the heavy traffic areas so we could get to them faster. She didn't ask any questions, probably sensing my trepidation. I kept blinking, willing myself to wake up from this nightmare. A million possible scenarios ran through my head, all of them horrific.

As soon as we got to the park, I jumped out of the car and ran straight for the monument. Yvonne called after me, but I didn't look back. Every part of me felt heavy as I pushed forward. There was something in Dylan's voice, a fearfulness I'd never heard before, that filled me up with dread.

I saw a few people gathered around and without thinking headed in that direction. In the distance, I heard ambulance sirens, but they were a way off yet. I broke through the people and gasped at what I saw. Dylan sat on the ground with Sam in his arms. He looked so . . . small. Both of them were beaten to a pulp and tears filled my eyes.

I fell onto the grass beside Dylan, hands moving over him in panic. "What happened?" My throat was heavy with emotion. It was just so wrong to see them both like this. They were two of the people I loved most in the world. Dylan was in such a daze he didn't even register my presence. He just rocked Sam back and forth as though willing him to open his eyes.

And Sam. My God. I could barely stand to look at him. There was a lesion above his eye that leaked blood all over his face, and the rest of him . . . the rest of him . . .

Yvonne let out a cry of shock when she finally caught up. Tears streamed down her cheeks as one of the onlookers approached. "I was sitting in my car when it happened," the man said, sounding shaken. "They were jogging, and a gang of teens ran out from behind the monument and attacked them. I called for help, but nobody's arrived yet. They were all wearing hoodies, so it was hard to make out their faces . . ."

I barely took in his words, too much shock in my system. I had my arms around Dylan, who still wouldn't let go of Sam. He held his small, battered body like he was terrified to let go. A terrible reality pushed at the edges of my brain, but I refused to acknowledge it.

The sirens blared as both the ambulance and the police arrived on the scene. Yvonne pulled me away from Dylan so that the paramedics could see to him and Sam. She wrapped her arms around me and whispered soothing noises in my ear.

I wanted to rage and scream.

I wanted to get whoever had done this and do the same to them.

I'd never felt so helpless, so enraged, and so heartbroken all at once. *This can't be real. It can't be happening.* Yvonne guided me over to her car, and we drove to the hospital in stunned silence. Once there, she called Dylan's dad and Sam's parents, doing her best to calmly relay for them what had happened. Both parties arrived at A&E in full panic, but nobody would tell us anything. Sam's mother was inconsolable. Nothing like this had ever happened to any of her children before. She just cried and cried, while her husband tried his best to soothe her.

We were told to stay in the waiting area until a doctor came out. About thirty minutes later, a female doctor came and informed Dylan's dad of his son's injuries. I listened intently, barely breathing, as she relayed the information: cracked ribs, a fractured nose and elbow, a concussion. With all that, I was surprised he was still conscious when I'd arrived at the scene. Only his dad was allowed in to see him. That would've frustrated me more if I wasn't still waiting with bated breath for news of Sam.

Hope was the only thing that kept me going, and every second that passed was a new agony. I kept hearing Dylan's words in my head.

I can't feel his pulse.

And the way he'd looked in Dylan's arms, so tiny and battered. A whirlwind of pain swept through me.

Finally, a doctor emerged, and as soon as I saw his face, I knew. Sam's mother let out an agonised wail.

His dad held her tight, but there were tears in his eyes, too.

And I, well, as soon as I heard the words, "Mrs Kennedy, Mr Kennedy, I'm so sorry . . ." something inside of me died. My candle, which had once burned bright, flickered out, leaving nothing but darkness.

My Sam was gone, and I would never, ever recover.

Seventeen

There's this thing called broken heart syndrome, where the emotional pain of losing a loved one leads to an actual medical condition. The surge of stress hormones causes a temporary disruption in the heart's normal pumping system, resulting in severe chest pain.

I felt like that was happening to me, because every part of my upper body ached.

My best friend, the boy who made me smile, who made me feel better whenever I was down, was gone. Just like that. Only yesterday we'd laughed in my bedroom and danced around to Fall Out Boy. It already felt like a lifetime ago.

I couldn't seem to reconcile the fact that I'd never see him again. That I had to live the rest of my life without him.

H-how . . .

How was I supposed to live the rest of my life without him?

I sat in the hospital waiting room, tears streaming down my face as I tried to make sense of how all this had happened so quickly. Yvonne placed a cup of tea and an oat bar in front of me, but I wasn't hungry. I felt like I might never be hungry again. All I felt was sick, empty, and hopeless.

When a nurse finally came to say I could go in and see Dylan, I walked down the corridor in a daze. He was being treated in a room with several other patients, but Tommy had pulled the curtain over. Dylan's dad came and hugged me tightly.

"That poor, poor boy," he rasped, speaking of Sam. "There's no justice in this world. None." He left to give us some privacy, and I brought my eyes to Dylan. He lay in bed, bandaged and hooked up to pain meds, his face devoid of colour.

"Evelyn," he breathed, and in that one word I heard all his guilt, pain, and anger. I heard his sadness. "I'm s-so sorry," he choked.

I didn't say anything for a moment, just came and sat down next to him. I took his hand in mine and squeezed it softly. A lone tear streamed down my face, its saltiness stinging my already raw skin. "Why? None of this is your fault."

"I brought him running with me, if I hadn't . . ." He paused, tears filling his eyes. As soon as I saw it, I started crying, too.

"Don't do that, don't blame yourself. The fault is at the hands of whoever did this."

Dylan's sadness turned to anger. "Jackson," he seethed. "As soon as I get of this hospital he's a dead man."

For a second, time stood still. "How do you—?"

"I saw him. He was one of them," Dylan gritted.

"Did you tell the Gardaí?"

"Yeah, but they'll be lucky if"—he paused and shifted his body, grimacing past the pain—"if I don't get to him first."

"Dylan, look at you. You're not fit to go after anyone," I said, thoughts racing. I couldn't believe a boy from our school was behind all this. Well, I mean, I *could* believe it, because he had a reputation for violence and was gunning for Dylan for months. But how could things escalate this far? How was *this* the logical outcome?

The man who witnessed the attack said there was a gang of them. A gang against two people. They didn't have a chance . . .

A memory flashed in my head, of Jackson at school with Kirsty whispering sweet nothings in his ear. Or was she whispering something else? I was certain she heard Dylan and Sam making plans to meet up for a run at the park. She could've easily forwarded this information to Jackson.

God, it didn't even bear thinking about, but I couldn't help it. The idea wormed its way into my brain, blackening my heart and soul. Was this her way of getting back at Dylan? A burning, fireball of anger lit inside me. I stood and walked straight out of the hospital room. Dylan called after me, but I didn't stop or turn back.

Like a raging bull, I walked all the way to the flats. I climbed the stairs to the very top floor where Kirsty lived and hammered on her door until it flung open. Her mam stood in front of me, a lit smoke hanging out of her mouth.

"What in the hell do you think you're doing banging my door like that?" she questioned in irritation, hand on hip.

"I'm looking for Kirsty," I answered, using all my might to keep my anger at bay until I saw her.

Her mam made a sound of displeasure and turned to call, "Kirsty, there's some young one at the door for you."

Kirsty emerged a moment later, eyes narrowing when she saw me. "What do *you* want?"

"Are you happy now? Do you feel better?" I fumed.

"Bitch, get the fuck away from here before I call my brothers out," she threatened.

"Jackson Keegan and his gang attacked Dylan and Sam this morning at the park. He and his buddies beat them so bad that Sam . . ." I choked, hardly able to say the words my grief was still so fresh. Finally, I blinked away the tears. Kirsty didn't deserve to see my pain. I pulled myself together, looked her dead in the eye and told her, "Sam died at the hospital."

Her mam, who was still standing in the doorway, put her hand to her mouth and gasped, while all the colour drained from Kirsty's face. "You're lying," she whispered, but I'd told her the truth, and she knew it. She looked like she'd seen a ghost. She looked like she was about to be sick and faint all at once. Gone was her tough exterior and catty attitude. Now she looked like she was realising the consequences of her meddling, the awful, horrific results.

"I hope you live a long life, Kirsty, and I hope that every single day you think of my best friend and know you had a hand in his death. I hope the guilt eats at you until there's nothing left."

With that I walked away. It wasn't enough. There was no justice in this. There never would be. Every year people were killed by violence in the city, but even if the criminals were sent to prison, it didn't bring the person you lost back.

Sam was gone, and I would never be the same without him.

I went home, got into bed, and cried so long my pillow was soaked through with tears. I cried until my throat ached. And then finally, with a hollow in my belly, I fell into an empty, dreamless sleep.

I refused to leave my bedroom for days. I was so consumed by grief I couldn't bring myself to go see Dylan at the hospital. I kept going over and over things in my head, wondering if I had done even one thing differently, maybe Sam would still be here.

If I'd said something to Kirsty at the lockers that day, if I'd tried to clear the air, would she still have told Jackson where Dylan and Sam would be that morning?

My brain was sore from my endlessly frantic thoughts. Once, I squeezed my eyes shut as tight as I could, like if I focused hard enough I could turn back time and prevent it all from happening.

My birthday came and went. I mostly slept through it, not wanting to think of how Sam was planning a surprise. It only hurt worse when I did.

I wasn't sure what day it was, or how long I'd been lost in my grief, when the door to my bedroom opened and someone stepped inside. I didn't look to see who it was. Didn't care. Then, Dylan's recognisable form crawled into bed behind me. I hadn't seen him since . . . since that day, but I knew he had one arm in a cast, his ribs were bandaged, and stitches sealed the deep cut on his temple. He pulled me close, wrapped his good arm around my middle and rested his head in the crook of my neck. He didn't speak, he just held me.

"They discharged me from the hospital an hour ago," he said, after a long few minutes of silence. "I came straight here."

I didn't say it, but I was glad he did. The fact that he was still breathing was the only thing keeping me going. Without him, the pieces I was made of would crumble and scatter. I wanted to tell him how much I appreciated his attempt at comfort, that I was sorry I hadn't come back to see him, but there was a block on my heart, on my voice. I was clogged up with anguish and didn't know how to expel the pain.

"Jackson was arrested," Dylan said, his voice so quiet it was barely a whisper.

I stilled. My heart jumped into my throat as I attempted to swallow it back down.

"When?" I asked. The word was painful to speak, but I had to know. I needed someone to blame, someone to despise. There was so much hate in my heart I didn't feel like myself anymore. I wasn't sure I'd ever be the same girl.

"This morning. They got three of the other lads who were with him, too. They're all eighteen, so they'll be tried as adults."

I swallowed and blinked away my tears. "Good."

"They'll go to prison for a long time," he went on. It sounded like he was saying it more to himself than to me. Like he was trying to convince himself it was for the best. I knew he'd wanted to go and get Jackson himself, but all that would achieve was him sharing a cell right along with him.

A sudden swell of sorrow gripped my body. The emotion was as familiar to me now as the back of my hand.

I pressed my face into the pillow to hide my crying, but it was no use. Feeling my body heave, Dylan pulled me closer and squeezed me tight. I tried to feel nothing, to quell the pain inside, because every second was agony.

"Ev," Dylan choked. He was grieving just the same as me.

"I wish I could go into a coma until this feeling fades," I whispered.

"You can't," he murmured, "but it will. You just have to go through each day until it does."

"I'm not sure I c-can," I said, voice cracking.

"You can. I know you can."

I knew Dylan understood grief. He'd lost his mam, so he completely understood the deathly ache in my heart. But he'd had time to say goodbye. And . . .

I closed my eyes for a second. I loved Dylan so much, but his optimism was futile, and ironic, since he'd always been the negative one. I would never get over this, and it hurt doubly to know he was waiting for the day when I would.

"My dad's gone to stay with my uncle in Galway for a little while," he said. "He'll be safer there."

I frowned and wiped at my tears. "What do you mean 'safer'?"

Dylan exhaled a tired sigh. I turned to look at him properly and saw his exhaustion mingled with fear. "The McCarthy's aren't going to be happy about their boys going to prison. It's only a matter of time before they figure out I was the one to give Jackson's name to the Gardaí."

At this I became incensed. I jumped out of bed and gestured angrily. "An innocent person died, how is that not enough for them?"

"These people aren't logical, Ev. It's all about optics, making sure everyone knows they're not to be fucked with."

I chocked a cry of pain. "This makes my head hurt."

Dylan blinked a few times, as though steeling himself, then reached out to grip my hand. "I'm going to America," he blurted and my stomach dropped.

This wasn't news I needed to be hearing right now. I didn't say anything, just stared at him, my expression empty.

"There's a department store in Los Angeles where my work has a branch," he continued. "I did a phone interview with the manager, and they offered me a job if I want it and—"

"Great. Good for you," I snipped.

Dylan frowned, "Don't be like that."

"Be like what? Sam's gone, and soon you'll be gone, too. I'm entitled to be any way I want."

"Ev, don't you understand? I want you to come with me. I always have."

I closed my eyes, because I didn't have the strength to have this argument with him again. I'd told him so many times I couldn't go, so why wouldn't he listen?

"You know I can't."

"Your gran would want you to."

I sat up now and crawled out of bed. My hair was a greasy mess, and I'd been wearing the same pyjamas for days. I went to stand by the window, hands on my hips as I stared him down. "I don't care what my gran would want. I don't want to go, so please drop the subject."

Dylan's face fell, and I despised myself for hurting him, but it had to be done. Swanning off to America together was a pipe dream. Maybe it was possible for him, but not for me. I had no money, no qualifications. Hell, I hadn't even finished school. Even if I wanted to go, there was no way I'd ever get a visa.

I told him as much, but he still wouldn't listen. He got down on his knees in front of me, gripped each of my hands in his and stared deep in my eyes.

"We'll sneak you in. Pretend you're going for a holiday and then just stay. I'll support you."

I let out a joyless laugh. Grief rendered me bitter. "Oh yeah, and then get deported when I'm found out. No thanks."

"That wouldn't happen. I'd figure out a way—"

"Look," I interrupted cuttingly. "I always knew you were going to leave, and now you have no reason to stay. Your dad's gone to his brother's, and he'll probably stay there. Plus, there's a gang out to get you. You couldn't stay even if you wanted to. I get that."

And I really did. It hurt worse than anything, but I understood. I wished I had the ability to be happy for him, but these days all I felt was misery and bitterness.

He raked a hand through his hair. It was growing out with a slight curl. "I need to get out of this place. Even before this happened, it suffocated me."

"I know. That's why I'm telling you to go."

He shook his head. "Ev, you're grieving, not thinking clearly."

I stared at him, so beautiful and sad as he knelt before me, and I knew I'd never love anyone in my life like I loved Dylan O'Dea. *He would always own my heart.* Always. But I wouldn't allow him to drown here. He was made for bigger things. I knew I wasn't, and that was why I had to make one of the hardest sacrifices I was sure I'd ever make. I had to push him onto that plane. I had to say goodbye. If I forced him to stay here, he'd waste away, never fulfil his potential. But out in the world . . .

Out in the world, he would shine.

The door to my room opened, and Yvonne walked in. She wasn't her usual groomed self, none of us were. Her hair was a knot on top of her head, and she wore no make-up. My aunt always wore immaculate make-up, but she hadn't so much as touched a tube of lipstick in days.

"Hey, you two," she said, not even questioning why Dylan was kneeling in front of me. Just like me, she'd lost her sparkle.

Sam had been the sparkle in all our lives, but we'd never realised how much until he was gone.

"I better go," Dylan murmured and stood. He didn't cast me another glance as he disappeared out the door. Yvonne emitted a soft sigh. She looked at me with such motherly concern I had to turn away.

"How are you?"

"Dylan's going to America," I said, avoiding her question.

"Oh." She was silent a long moment before she asked, "And how do you feel about that?"

Like the entire world is coming to an end.

"It doesn't matter how I feel. He has to go. If he stays, those boys who killed Sam will come after him again. It's only a matter of time."

She chewed on her lip, like she didn't know how to respond to that. There was no motherly advice, no way of turning this lemon in lemonade. I followed her out to the kitchen and watched as she put the kettle on. She exhaled tiredly, not looking at me as she spoke softly, "Sam's funeral is tomorrow."

A lump formed in my throat. A funeral was too final. I didn't know what to say, so I simply turned and went back inside my room. Yvonne came and placed a sandwich and sugary cup of tea on my bedside table.

"You can wear my black dress, if you like."

I shot her a thankful look, both for the food and the offer of the dress. "Sam always loved that one," I said.

She gave a sad smile. "He said it made me look like Grace Kelly."

"You do look like her. We could be related. She had Irish roots," I said, forcing a smile in return.

"Maybe that's where we got our blonde hair," Yvonne replied and slipped off her shoes.

She climbed into bed beside me, and we ate in quiet contemplation. The sandwich tasted like nothing, all food was the same, but I ate it nonetheless. When I was done I turned over and went back to sleep.

When I woke later, Yvonne had gone to work. It was dark out and the moon shone through the open curtains. There was something about the light that made me feel sad, so I got up and pulled them closed. I walked restlessly around my bedroom.

I considered taking a shower when my phone lit up with a call. The screen read 'Mam' and my stomach dropped. Why was she calling again? What did she want?

Deciding to get it over with, I picked up the phone and answered.

"Hello." My voice was staid, flat.

"Evelyn, it's Mam," she greeted. Her tone was saccharine and maybe a little tipsy, which explained her calling at such an unsociable hour. I knew the sweetness was a front. She wanted something, that's why she was putting it on.

"I know that."

She cleared her throat, obviously thrown by my hostility. Usually, I was nice, even though she didn't deserve it. But now, in this post-Sam reality, I could give two fucks about being nice. Nice didn't get you anywhere in this cold, brutal world where the best things were taken, and you had no way to ever get them back.

Mam's voice grew softer now. "I heard about little Sammy, Evelyn. I'm so sorry."

"No, you're not."

"Don't say that." She sounded offended.

"Don't pretend to care."

"Of course, I care. I've been trying to call you for weeks, but I only ever get your voicemail. I wanted to tell you I'm coming home."

"Why would that mean anything to me?"

"Because I'm your mother," she replied, hurt.

"That didn't stop you from leaving the first time. If you're coming back, fine, but don't expect a warm welcome from me." With that, I hung up, pissed. It was probably my anger that fuelled me to walk into the bathroom and get in the shower. There was nothing like a bit of cold, hard fury to finally snap you out of melancholy.

I was still awake when Yvonne got home, since I'd slept most of the day.

"Oh, you're up," she said. She sounded exhausted.

"Yep. I had a shower and everything. Also, Mam called."

Yvonne grimaced, but she didn't look surprised. "Yeah, she um, called me, too."

"What did she say?"

"She and her boyfriend have broken up. She's also been fired from her job. She wouldn't say why, but I suspect she was caught stealing."

So that was why she was so eager to return home. The police were probably looking for her over there.

"I don't want anything to do with her," I said firmly.

"No, I don't blame you," Yvonne replied, and it threw me. Normally, my aunt would've encouraged me to give Mam a chance, see where things went. But not now. The loss of Sam had affected her just as much as it did me. She wasn't so forgiving anymore; her leniency reserves were all dried up.

"Where are they burying Sam?" I asked.

"Glasnevin," Yvonne replied. "We can drive over in the morning."

I chewed on my lip, still feeling restless. "No, I'll meet you there. I have, um, something I need to do."

"It's four a.m., Ev. Go back to sleep. Whatever you need to do can wait."

"This can't," I replied as I threw on some jeans and a T-shirt. I opened the wardrobe and pulled out Yvonne's black dress and some shoes. I threw them in a bag and also grabbed Yvonne's wheelie grocery carrier. I'd always teased her for having it, but right then it was exactly what I needed.

"Where are you going?"

"Just to the roof to do some gardening," I replied.

"Okay, well, don't work too hard. I'll see you in the morning."

"Yeah, see you then," I said and hurried out the door.

After days of endless misery, it felt good to have a purpose.

When I reached the roof, I unlocked the metal storage box where I kept all my gardening tools and got to work. I cut, dug, and pulled out every single plant from the soil. My sunflowers and lilacs, my wildflowers and echinacea. Now that the sun was up, they had all opened for the day. For the final time. There was something sad and beautiful about that. Maybe they would go wherever Sam was, surround him in colour and pretty scents.

Most of my flowers were diurnal, which meant they closed at night to keep unwanted bugs away, but opened in the day to attract their little buzzy friends.

Melancholy clutched my heart, because I didn't think I'd garden again. I didn't have it in me. I realised that my ability to grow was closely connected to my affinity for positivity and hope. But those things didn't live here anymore. They weren't a part of me anymore either.

When I was done, Yvonne's wheelie carrier was full to the brim, fit to burst, while my allotment lay bare, a barren wasteland. It took a while to get down the stairs with all my cargo, but I just about managed it. I caught a bus to Glasnevin, and asked the caretaker for directions to Sam's grave.

I stood before it, nothing but an empty rectangle in the ground and thought, this wasn't how it was supposed to be. It just . . .

. . . wasn't right.

A tear fell down my cheek, as I pictured life how it should've been. Sam and me getting a flat together, him pursuing a career in singing, while I saved up to open my own florist. It was a picturesque world, one that would never exist for us.

I sniffled, blew my nose, and wiped away my tears with the back of my hand. After clearing out my entire allotment, I was already exhausted, but my work wasn't done yet. Not by a long shot. Pulling on my gloves, I got started.

"Never seen something like that before," the caretaker said with a whistle when I was finished. "We've had our fair share of extravagant displays, but nothing like this."

My eyes traced the medley of colours and a small sliver of peace sealed my heart. Sam would've loved it. He was nothing if not ostentatious. The bright yellows, deep reds, and vibrant purples made my chest swell with pride. The last flowers I would ever grow paid tribute to my lost friend.

It was all I had to give him.

I gathered the last of my things and went to the visitor bathrooms to change. Once I was dressed, I went back out and saw a lone figure standing by Sam's grave. He wasn't dressed for a funeral, but still, I'd never seen Shane look so broken.

"Does it hurt?" I asked, coming to stand next to him.

Shane glanced at me then back to my flower display. "I could ask you the same question."

"Like a bastard," I said, quiet.

Shane grimaced. "Guess we're in the same boat then." A few moments of silence elapsed before he gestured to the display, "This your doing?"

"Yes."

"He'd a loved it." His voice was mildly choked and I frowned. I'd thought it was only sex between them, but maybe I was wrong. Maybe it was more than that.

"You're right, he would."

"I think I loved him," Shane blurted, and his confession truly surprised me.

I stared at him a moment, then cleared my throat. "Did you?"

"You don't have to sound so fuckin' cynical. I'm capable of love."

"Well, you'll forgive me for thinking otherwise."

He arched a brow. "Will I?"

"It's a figure of speech."

He ran a hand over his jaw. "Yeah well, I'm gonna m-miss him." There was a quaver of emotion in his voice and for some reason it set me off, too.

"There'll never be another one like him," I said, choked.

"Nope. Little shit was one of a kind."

Silence fell between us, and I saw some people start to arrive at the cemetery. I couldn't see Sam's parents yet, but I hoped they'd appreciate my tribute. Flowers meant life to me. Vibrancy. Hope. And that had been Sam. He'd been such a vibrant and vital part of my life. For a long time, he and Yvonne had been my everything. And now . . . I shook my head. I didn't want this day to happen. I couldn't be here and say goodbye.

"Why were you so horrible to him?" I asked Shane. "I mean, before you got together."

It took him a moment to answer. "Guess I hated the fact that I liked him, so I lashed out."

"Makes sense," I said, because it did. That didn't mean I'd ever forgive Shane for his treatment of Sam in the beginning. Maybe we shared a connection of loving the same person, but we'd never be friends.

"Will you come out now?" I asked. I wondered if the loss would make him a better person. Surely some good might come of Sam's death. *It had to.*

"I don't know. Maybe."

I looked at him, my expression sincere. "You should. It's no kind of life hiding like that."

Shane studied me a moment, like he was thinking about what I said. I wondered if he agreed. I reached out for a second and squeezed his shoulder. "I'm glad he had you. I'm glad he got to experience love before he went."

Shane visibly swallowed then nodded. His eyes shone, and I thought he might cry, but he turned and walked away. I stood by the grave as more and more people arrived. There were so many of our neighbours from the Villas, kids from school. Sometimes it felt like Sam and I only had each other, like I was the only one who really knew him, but he'd obviously made an impression on lots of others, too.

Yvonne arrived and came to stand next to me. She wore sunglasses and a dark-coloured blouse.

"You look so grown," she commented.

"It's just the dress."

She shook her head, sounding sad when she said, "No, it isn't."

246

I knew what she meant. Losing Sam had made me grow up much faster than I was supposed to, and all in the wrong order. Amy and Conor arrived; each gave me a hug and stood close. I was glad for them. I needed their strength.

I was distracted when Dylan came and took my hand in his. After our conversation yesterday, the gesture was unexpected. I knew he'd be pissed at me, but I also knew his heart. He loved me. Was living for me. He understood how much losing Sam was wrecking me, and his empathy and love was something I'd clung to. In a way, he'd also lost a friend, a brother, so I knew his heart ached as well. Together.

Today we'd grieve together.

Eighteen

"The display is beautiful," Dylan murmured in my ear. He recognised the flowers as my work instantly. I knew he would.

Sam's mother came and hugged me for a long time. She didn't say anything, because she was crying, but the hug expressed her gratitude for how pretty I'd made Sam's grave. I swallowed, trying so hard not to cry, too. Although today, surely it was inevitable.

Afterward, there was food and drinks at Sam's flat, but I only stayed for a short while. As I left, someone came behind me and softly touched my shoulder.

"You're leaving?" Dylan asked.

I turned and he gazed down at me, his expression full of warmth, full of empathy. And guilt. His guilt was misplaced, but I didn't know how to stop him from feeling it.

"Yes, I just need some rest," I replied quietly.

"Can I come with you?"

In this eyes, I saw how much he needed me, so I nodded, and we continued to my flat. Once there, I went into my bedroom and Dylan followed. I stood by my bed and looked at him, still so injured. I wondered what it was like to grieve while your body was in so much physical pain at the same time.

His dark blue gaze held mine, communicated a depth I wasn't sure we could ever put into words. I stepped forward and carefully undressed him. I slid his blazer down his shoulders, unbuttoned his shirt. I carefully peeled away each layer until I saw his bruised and battered body.

When I was done, Dylan watched while I slid off my dress, until I stood in only my underwear. I stepped in front of him, kissed one of his cheeks and then the other. I kissed his neck and his collarbone, his breastplate and the white gauze around his ribs. I ran my fingers along the cast on his arm and pressed my lips to the stitches at his forehead. All the while, he seemed to hold his breath.

"You were right," I whispered.

He stared down at me. "About what?"

"About this place. It did turn me hard, only it happened a lot sooner than you predicted."

"That's not true. You just feel that way because you're grieving."

I shook my head. "Losing Sam opened my eyes to everything you've been trying to tell me all along. This place is horrible, and it's full of horrible people. If we didn't live here, you wouldn't have bullies coming after you. There wouldn't be people who are so empty inside that the only way for them to feel anything is to beat a person until they aren't a person anymore."

I paused and tears streamed down my face. "If we didn't live here, Dylan, Sam would still be alive. That's someone I'll think about every day for the rest of my life."

Dylan ran a hand down his face. In his expression, I saw his regret, saw how he wished he'd never opened my eyes to the lowliness of our existence. His regret was pointless, of course, because I would've found out for myself anyway. I just would've been less prepared.

He pulled me to him and hugged me tight. He knew there was nothing he could say to make it better, nothing he could do to take back all the things he'd been trying to make me understand this whole time.

The world could be ugly or beautiful, depending on where you found yourself. You could create a little beauty in an ugly place, but in the end, the ugliness would eat it up.

That's what happened to Sam.

And that's what was happening to me.

There was a crack in me now, and someday it was going to expand and swallow me whole.

Dylan laid me down on the bed, pulled the covers over our bodies, and kissed me until my lips were sore. He kissed every inch of me, temporarily easing a small piece of the pain. I repaid him in kind, trying to memorise how he gasped in pleasure, how handsome he looked when he gazed at me with love. I did it because soon he'd be gone, and these memories would be all I had left.

I woke up early the next morning to movement. Dylan stood at the foot of my bed, awkwardly trying to dress himself.

"You're going," I said, a statement, not a question.

Dylan nodded. "I have a check-up at the hospital, and then I have to visit the passport office."

"Oh," I said, sitting up and pulling the covers around me. All of a sudden, I felt so cold.

Dylan stared at me a long moment. "You're not coming with me, are you?"

I shook my head sadly, my voice no more than a whisper. "No. I'm sorry."

His expression was tender yet fierce. "Don't be. Life's too short to live in regret, Ev. I want you to come with me because I'm selfish, but you need to do what's best for you. And if that means staying here and finishing school, taking care of your gran, then that's what you need to do."

The way he said it, so full of compassion and love, made another piece of my already broken heart break off. I got out of bed, stood before him and placed my hands on each of his shoulders.

"You're going to thrive out there, do you know that?" I said, sniffling.

"I'm going try my best," he replied, eyes searching mine.

"You won't try, you'll do. I know you will."

"I'll miss you," he said, a catch in his voice. Those three little words held all the emotion of a hundred lifetimes, and we were both in danger of drowning under the weight of them.

"I'll miss you, too," I croaked and pulled him into a hug. Tears streamed down my face. I'd cried so much these last few days, I was surprised there were any more left in me.

"And don't you ever come back here," I said, squeezing him tight. "If you do I'll never speak to you again."

He didn't comment on the irony of my words. Instead he pulled back to look at me, his expression thoughtful. "This isn't the end for us. I promise. This is just the in-between. I'll find you in the after."

Something in me hoped it was true, because it made it easier to accept him leaving. But another part of me said it was wishful thinking, just my heart clouding my head with foolish notions. Sure, we could try to reconnect, try to stay in touch, but what was the point when I was never leaving this place? I'd only drag him down, and he deserved to fly high.

When I finally let go, I wiped away my tears and mustered a smile just for him.

"Then I'll see you in the after."

The story continues in book #2, *How the Light Gets In*.

He came back to me 16 minutes and 59 seconds into Beethoven's Symphony no. 7.

We parted amid tragedy, so it seemed poetic. Dylan O'Dea, my childhood sweetheart, had once meant everything to me. Now we were strangers, and honestly, after eleven years I never thought I'd see him again.

I lived in the world of the average, of getting paid by the hour and budgeting to make ends meet. But Dylan, he lived in the world of wealth and success. He'd achieved the great things I always suspected he would. The dissatisfaction he'd felt as a teenager had obviously been an excellent motivator.

He started a business from scratch, pioneered a brand, and created perfumes adored by women across the globe. I was just one of the people who'd been there before. Now he was living his best life in the after.

And me, well, I'd been in a dark place for a while. Slowly but surely, I was letting the light back in, but there was something missing. I was an unfinished sentence with an ellipsis at the end. And maybe, if I was brave enough to take the chance, Dylan could be my happy ending.

How the Light Gets In is the concluding instalment in L.H. Cosway's Cracks duet.

About the Author

L.H. Cosway lives in Dublin, Ireland. Her inspiration to write comes from music. Her favourite things in life include writing stories, vintage clothing, dark cabaret music, food, musical comedy, and of course, books. She thinks that imperfect people are the most interesting kind. They tell the best stories.

Find L.H. Cosway online!

www.lhcoswayauthor.com
www.twitter.com/LHCosway
www.facebook.com/LHCosway
www.instagram.com/l.h.cosway

L.H. Cosway's *HEARTS* Series

Praise for *Six of Hearts* (Book #1)

"This book was sexy. Man was it hot! Cosway writes sexual tension so that it practically sizzles off the page." - A. Meredith Walters, New York Times & USA Today Bestselling Author.

"Six of Hearts is a book that will absorb you with its electric and all-consuming atmosphere." - Lucia, Reading is my Breathing.

"There is so much "swoonage" in these pages that romance readers will want to hold this book close and not let go." - Katie, Babbling About Books.

Praise for *Hearts of Fire* (Book #2)

"This story holds so much intensity and it's just blazing hot. It created an inferno of emotions inside me." - Patrycja, Smokin' Hot Book Blog.

"I think this is my very favorite LH Cosway romance to date. Absolutely gorgeous." - Angela, Fiction Vixen.

"Okay we just fell in love. Complete and utter beautiful book love. You know the kind of love where you just don't want a book to finish. You try and make it last; you want the world to pause as you read and you

want the story to go on and on because you're not ready to let it go." - Jenny & Gitte, Totally Booked.

Praise for *King of Hearts* (Book #3)

"Addictive. Consuming. Witty. Heartbreaking. Brilliant--King of Hearts is one of my favourite reads of 2015!" - Samantha Young, New York Times, USA Today and Wall Street Journal bestselling author.

"I was looking for a superb read, and somehow I stumbled across an epic one." - Natasha is a Book Junkie.

"5+++++++ Breathtaking stars! Outstanding. Incredible. Epic. Overwhelmingly romantic and poignant. There's book love and in this case there's BOOK LOVE." - Jenny & Gitte, Totally Booked.

Praise for *Hearts of Blue* (Book #4)

"From its compelling characters, to the competent prose that holds us rapt cover to cover, this is a book I could not put down." - Natasha is a Book Junkie.

"Devoured it in one sitting. Sexy, witty, and fresh. Their love was not meant to be, their love should never

work, but Lee and Karla can't deny what burns so deep and strong in their hearts. Confidently a TRSoR recommendation and fave!"- The Rock Stars of Romance.

"WOW!!! It's hard to find words right now, I don't think the word LOVE even makes justice or can even describe how much I adored this novel. Karla handcuffed my senses and Lee stole my heart."- Dee, Wrapped Up In Reading

Praise for *Thief of Hearts* (Book #5)

"This is easily one of our favorite romances by L.H. Cosway. We were consumed by the brilliant slow-burn and smoldering student/teacher forbidden storyline with layers of uncontainable, explosive raw emotions and genuine heart." – The Rock Stars of Romance.

"I was in love with this couple and was championing their relationship from the start." – I Love Book Love

"One of my fave reads of this year. Mind-blowing and thrilling, let this story sweep you off your feet!" – Aaly and the Books.

Books by L.H. Cosway

Contemporary Romance
Painted Faces
Killer Queen
The Nature of Cruelty
Still Life with Strings
Showmance

The Cracks Duet
A Crack in Everything (#1)
How the Light Gets in (#2)

The Hearts Series
Six of Hearts (#1)
Hearts of Fire (#2)
King of Hearts (#3)
Hearts of Blue (#4)
Thief of Hearts (#5)
Hearts on Air (#6)

The Rugby Series with Penny Reid
The Hooker & the Hermit (#1)
The Player & the Pixie (#2)
The Cad & the Co-ed (#3)

Urban Fantasy
Tegan's Blood (The Ultimate Power Series #1)
Tegan's Return (The Ultimate Power Series #2)
Tegan's Magic (The Ultimate Power Series #3)
Tegan's Power (The Ultimate Power Series #4)

Made in the USA
Columbia, SC
06 February 2018